LOOKING FOR LOVE?

Your perfect match is waiting
for you within these pages!

As you read, you'll meet lots of amazing guys,
but only one will steal your heart.

How will you find him? Simply make a choice
at the end of each chapter. Your decisions
will lead you to the guy who's right for you.

So pack your bags, and board the train that will
take you to your gorgeous beachside destination.
Because a summer of love awaits . . .

OTHER BOOKS YOU MAY ENJOY

FOLLOW *Your* HEART

summer love

jill santopolo

SPEAK
AN IMPRINT OF PENGUIN GROUP (USA)

SPEAK

Published by the Penguin Group
Penguin Group (USA) LLC
375 Hudson Street
New York, New York 10014

USA * Canada * UK * Ireland * Australia
New Zealand * India * South Africa * China

penguin.com
A Penguin Random House Company

First published in the United States of America by Speak,
an imprint of Penguin Group (USA) LLC, 2014

LIBRARY OF CONGRESS CATALOGING-IN-PUBLICATION DATA
Santopolo, Jill.
Summer love / Jill Santopolo.
pages cm.—(Follow your heart)
Summary: "A unique romance novel whereby readers are prompted to choose
how to proceed with the plot, leading them to one of eleven different love
interests and thirteen possible endings"—Provided by publisher.
ISBN 978-0-14-751092-1 (pbk.)
1. Plot-your-own stories. [1. Love—Fiction. 2. Dating (Social customs)—Fiction.
3. Plot-your-own stories.]
I. Title. PZ7.S23828Su 2014 [Fic]—dc23 2013045024

Speak ISBN 978-0-14-751092-1

Printed in the United States of America
1 3 5 7 9 10 8 6 4 2

For Casa Vin Santo

YOU LEAN YOUR HEAD against the train window and watch the ocean as it whizzes by. You've listened to the summer playlist you created on your iPod twice through already, and there's still another half hour until your stop. Your cousin Tasha pokes you in the shoulder.

"Twizzler?" she asks, loud enough that you can hear her over your music. You pop an earbud out of your ear and take the candy she's offering.

"Thanks," you say, before you chomp down.

Tasha grabs one herself. "So," she says, "I never asked. Did you get everything you wanted for your birthday?"

You chew as you think about your sweet sixteen, which was six—no, seven—days ago. "The party was great," you say. "And this beach trip, just you and me, is the most awesome gift ever. But I guess there was one thing I'd been hoping for."

You sigh and take another bite of Twizzler, but Tasha won't let you off that easy.

"Which was . . . ?" she asks, raising an eyebrow.

You pull your hair over your eyes so you don't have to look at her when you say it. "I was hoping Tyler Grant was going to kiss me."

You tuck your hair back behind your ear and look at Tasha. Even though you both live in the same city, you go to different schools, and she's two years older, so she doesn't know all of your friends.

"Is that the hot ginger?" she asks. "The one who was dancing with you at the end of your party?"

You shake your head. "No. Tyler's the tall one with the hipster glasses. The one who didn't really dance much at all."

Tasha runs her Twizzler back and forth across her lips as she thinks. "Oh! The one in the green shirt! I remember him." She gives you an appraising look. "You can do way better than that."

"I don't know," you reply, finishing the last of your candy. "He's really cool. And funny—like in a sarcastic way."

Tasha puts her hand on your arm. "Trust me, cuz.

You can do better." Then her face lights up. "I have an idea! Since this is your birthday present beach weekend, you should make it your mission to get a birthday kiss from the cutest boy you can find."

"I'm not sure," you say, mostly because you're afraid you might fail at this mission, and then it would be doubly disappointing.

"How about . . . you don't have to kiss him. You can if you want, but your mission will be to flirt with the cutest boy you can find."

You smile. That sounds doable.

"Deal," you say, holding your hand out to Tasha.

"Deal," she says back, shaking it.

Then you both start laughing, and Tasha says, "I still bet you can find someone to kiss, though."

You make what you hope is a coy face, and then pop your earbud back into your ear. Secretly, you wish Tasha is right and you can find someone to kiss this weekend. But only time will tell.

✳

TWENTY minutes later, Tasha shakes your shoulder, jolting you out of a very real dream in which you were kissing Tyler Grant, and shoves your duffel bag at you. "Next stop is us! We've got to get our stuff together!"

You blink a few times, and then throw your magazines, empty smoothie cup, iPod, and sweatshirt into a tote and stand with a bag on each arm. The train slows to a stop as the conductor calls out the station name, and you follow Tasha and about a billion other people out of the train toward the beach.

The minute you get onto the train platform, Tasha is scanning the parking lot for Jade, her best friend and soon-to-be college roommate. Tasha and Jade have spent every summer together since Tasha's parents bought a beach house the year she turned eight.

You see Jade sitting in the front seat of a convertible, next to her brother Dex. But before you can point it out, Jade yells "Tash!" and then stands up on the seat. "Over here!"

You and Tasha head to Jade and Dex's car, toss your stuff in the trunk, and jump over the sides into the backseat.

"Hey," Dex says to you. "Happy birthday!"

"You, too," you answer. Dex's birthday is a day before yours—a year and a day, actually— something you learned ages ago, when you and your parents came for a visit. "Do anything fun?"

He shrugs. "You know, the usual." You don't know what "the usual" means, but you're too caught up in looking at Dex's face to ask. His hair is the same curly blond it's always been, but in the last year he seems to have grown cheekbones—and a beard. Really, it's just light blond stubble across his cheeks and chin, but it looks very manly. You think about your plan and wonder if Dex is the guy to flirt with. Maybe even kiss. Before you can decide he says, "So, where to, ladies? Want to come to the country club with Jade and me, or should I drop you somewhere else?"

Tasha looks at you. "Your choice," she says. "We can go with Dex, or we can head to my parents' place and unpack. Whatever you want."

Turn to page 7 if you decide
to go to the country club with Dex.

- - - - -

Turn to page 13 if you'd
rather head home first.

DEX looks at you through the rearview mirror with blue eyes that are so dark they're almost navy. "So?" he asks.

Even though you're still a little tired from the train trip and being woken up right before the station was called, you decide you might as well make the most of your birthday weekend. "To the country club!" you say.

Dex floors it, and Jade whoops as she takes the elastic out of her hair and lets it whip around her head. "I love the summer!" she shouts into the wind.

You lean back against the seat and let the sun soak into your skin. Dex is going too fast for you all to have a real conversation anyway.

He pulls up to the front of the country club, and a valet comes around to open the car door for you and Jade. There's another one on Tasha and Dex's side, opening their door.

"Will we have the car all afternoon?" the valet on Dex's side asks him.

"Not sure yet," Dex answers. "I'm at the ladies' beck and call today." His eyes flick over to you, and you smile. Then the four of you head inside to the dining room.

"I'm so hungry I could eat, like, six salads," Jade says.

Dex rolls his eyes. "Jade, you wouldn't be so starving if you actually ate breakfast."

"A cup of coffee totally counts as a normal breakfast, right?" Jade turns to you and Tasha.

You shrug. "I usually eat cereal," you say.

"And I usually eat yogurt," Tasha adds. "But if that's what you want to eat for breakfast, I think that's totally fine, Jade."

"See?" Jade says to Dex.

You've made it to the maître d' stand, and the four of you stop.

"Would you like a table outside or inside?" the maître d' asks.

"Absolutely outside!" Jade says, before anyone else can answer.

You can't help but smile at her summer excitement as you follow her, Tasha, and Dex to the patio. You sit down under an umbrella, overlooking the pool and the tennis courts, and very quickly there's a glass of iced tea sweating in your hand and Cobb salad sitting in front of you. Dex is next to you with his own iced tea, and a chicken sandwich on his plate. He's very involved in eating. Tasha gives you a look that very clearly means: Talk to him! And so you clear your throat and you do.

"So, um, Dex, do you have any special plans for the summer?" you ask him.

He nods as he finishes swallowing. "Well, I'm going to work in my dad's law office out here—they have a satellite office because two of the partners have summer houses nearby—and then I'm going to play as much tennis as possible."

Tennis! You'd almost forgotten how good he was at tennis. You're pretty good, too, actually, but he doesn't know that. He's never seen you play. And you've never talked about it, either, because you hate sounding braggy. "Oh right," you say, "you won the junior tennis tournament for the club last summer when I was here."

He nods, taking a sip of iced tea. "I'm hoping

for a repeat, but this time with the adult tennis tournament. They won't let me play with the kids anymore."

You laugh. "Does that mean you're officially a grown-up now?"

"Oh, absolutely," he says, with mock sincerity.

You look over at Tasha, who's listening to Jade talk about colors for their dorm room, and Tasha gives you a subtle nod. Clearly you're on the right track with this flirting business.

"So now that you're a grown-up," you say, "does that mean that you, um, read the newspaper every morning?"

"And brew my own coffee, and wear a tie to work, and walk the dog," he answers.

"You doink." Jade stops her discussion about whether hunter green and navy blue would make their dorm room feel too dark to admonish her brother. "We don't even have a dog!"

Dex laughs, and you do, too.

"Guess according to Jade I'm not quite a grown-up yet."

"Oh, little brother," Jade tells him, "even when you're ninety-nine and I'm a hundred, I'll still call you out on being a doink."

"Do you see what I have to deal with?" Dex says to you.

"Well, I don't think you're a doink," you answer. "You're not at all doink-ish to me."

Dex turns to Tasha. "Why don't you bring her around more often?"

You try not to smile too wide, but clearly you're not so bad at flirting. Just as you take another bite of your salad, three guys and three girls in tennis whites come over.

"Dex!" one of the guys says. "Any chance you're free this afternoon? Jed and Cali bailed, and we need two more for mixed doubles."

"Jade?" one of the girls says. "Any interest in playing against us with your brother?"

Jade wrinkles her nose. "The only kind of 'serve' I plan to think about today is the kind where the guy at the pool brings me lemonade while I read magazines and get tan."

"Well, I can play," Dex says, "even if my sister won't."

Tasha raises an eyebrow at you, then says, "I don't know if she's mentioned it, Dex, but that girl sitting to your right has a killer backhand."

The tennis guy who spoke to Dex first looks at

you, intrigued. "You play?" he asks.

You nod. "I'm not as good as Dex, but I'm on my school's tennis team."

Dex cocks his head at you. "How did I not know that?" he asks.

You shrug.

"Well, you want to play with us this afternoon? Did you bring tennis clothes?" He takes another sip of his iced tea.

You do have some tennis clothes in your bag in the car. . . .

"Or you can come hang by the pool with us," Jade says, "if you'd rather relax. You can always play tomorrow."

Turn to page 29 if you agree to play a game of mixed doubles with Dex.

- - - - -

Or turn to page 23 if you'd rather hang by the pool with Tasha and Jade.

AS cute as Dex has become, you can't stop thinking about the time he peed in his pants the summer he turned seven because he didn't want to run to the bathroom in the middle of the Fourth of July fireworks. And how he once gave himself a hickey on his arm just to see if he could. And the way he used to tease you because you didn't like swimming in the ocean. There was just too much history here. Kissing Dex would be like kissing your cousin. Besides, you're feeling kind of grimy from your train ride and wouldn't mind washing your face and unpacking for the weekend before starting on your flirt hunt.

"I think maybe a trip back to the house would be best," you tell Tasha, "as long as you really don't mind."

"Not at all," she says. And then turns to Dex, "To the house, sir!"

Jade laughs. "Dex getting his license is the best thing that ever happened to me. Now I have a chauffeur to take me everywhere!"

"Hey, watch it, or I'll leave you all on the side of the road," Dex says, staring straight ahead.

"Do that, and I'm sure we'll find some cute boys to take us where we want to go, right, girls?" Jade turns around to wink at you and Tasha.

"Absolutely!" Tasha says.

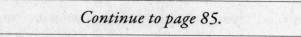

Continue to page 85.

YOU drop your stuff in the yellow room, change into your skimpiest bikini for maximum tanning potential, and head out to the pool, carrying a stash of magazines, a bottle of water, and a cover-up in a tote. Tasha's already there in her teeniest suit with a *Teen Vogue* balanced in just the right way so it won't give her a weird magazine-shaped tan line.

"I've got the perfect quiz for you," Tasha says. It's 'What Literary Leading Man Is Your True Love?'"

You know this is just going to lead to her bugging you about finding a guy cuter than Tyler Grant this weekend, so instead of playing along, you say, "How about you take the quiz?"

Tasha shakes her head. "It's for you! It's your birthday weekend!"

"How about you go first, then me?" you ask her, already plotting to distract her with something else after she's done with the quiz.

She lets out a long-suffering sigh. "Fine," she says, holding the magazine out to you. "Ask me."

"Okay," you say, reading from the quiz. "Is a man's most important quality his: (a) intelligence, (b) loyalty, (c) sexiness, or (d) passion."

"Hmm," Tasha says, closing her eyes and thinking. "Can I say all of the above?"

You shake your head. "No, you cannot say all of the above! Then all the Literary Leading Men will be your true love, and you can only have one!"

Tasha opens her eyes and sits up. "Do you really think so? Do you think there's just one?"

"For this quiz there is," you tell her, laughing. But you realize she's not laughing with you.

"I'm serious," she says. "I mean, it's fun to flirt and kiss and dance at parties and go out for coffee after school and stuff, but do you think there's just one perfect match for all of us?"

You chew your lip as you think. It's not something you've really considered before. Finally, you give her your most honest answer, which is, "I don't know."

Tasha lies back in the chaise lounge. "Yeah," she

says. "I don't know, either." She looks down at her fingers. "Do you want to give me a manicure?" she asks. "And when mine dries, I'll give you one."

"Sure," you tell her. "What color do you want?"

She leans over and rummages around in the tote bag on the right side of her chair. "Yellow," she says, handing you a bottle of metallic polish. "Perfect for summer."

You scooch your chaise lounge closer to hers and start carefully polishing Tasha's nails. Her eyes are closed again, and her chin is tipped up so she won't get a neck-crease tan line.

"I think tonight we should go somewhere to find boys," she says sleepily. "Maybe they'll be intelligent and loyal and . . . what where the other ones?"

"Sexy and passionate," you tell her.

"Yeah, those."

"Are you falling asleep?" you ask her, as you finish polishing her pinky.

"Mm, maybe," she says.

"I'm not polishing your nails if you're sleeping," you tell her. "That's too weird."

Tasha's eyes snap open. "I'm up!" she says. "But I'm tired." She looks at her nails. You've done one coat of yellow on all of them. "Maybe stop there," she says, sheepishly. "I can do a second coat later. We got up really early this morning. Would it be all right if I took a nap?"

You smile at your cousin. "Go for it," you say. "I'll wake you if anything superexciting happens."

You shove your chaise lounge back to its original position and start to read the rest of Tasha's *Teen Vogue*. You haven't gotten all that far, though, when you hear a dog barking. At first you ignore it, but the dog won't stop. And it sounds as if it's getting closer. Could the dog have run away? Does it need rescuing? You decide to investigate, so you get up off your chair, pull on your cover-up, and walk down the path along the side of the house until you reach the gate that separates the front yard of the house from the road beyond it. And then you see him.

There's a dog, sure, a supercute Dalmatian who's barking his head off. But also a tall, broad-shouldered guy with dark wavy hair and sideburns. He's wearing a white V-neck T-shirt and plaid shorts that are half cool and half dorky. And he's got leather flip-flops on his feet.

You clear your throat, and he looks at you. "Is everything okay?" you ask. "I mean, with your dog?"

Sideburns smiles and looks a little embarrassed.

"Sorry. Gonzo's a little crazy. He barks at cars. Always. It makes walking him a huge pain in the butt. But I love him anyway."

He bends down and rubs Gonzo's head. "Don't I love you, boy?" he asks. The dog barks in response.

"Barking at cars," you say. "That's some talent."

Sideburns laughs. "Seems like he's got another one, too."

"Oh yeah?" you ask. "What's that?"

He scratches the back of his head, and you think maybe his cheeks are turning a little pink, but it's hard to tell. "Finding pretty girls?" he says, almost as if it's a question.

You can't help but laugh.

"Lame line," he says, definitely blushing this time. "I know."

Somehow the lame pickup line has made him even more endearing. You stick your hand through the wide space between the rails of the gate and introduce yourself.

He slides his hand into yours and shakes it. "Nice to meet you," he says. "I'm Nikhil. But most people call me Nik."

His hand is warm and soft—big, too.

"Are you here for the summer?" he asks.

He lets go of your hand, and you shake your head. "Just for the weekend," you tell him. "My cousin Tasha's going to be here all summer, though. This is her parents' house. She's asleep back there by the pool."

"Ah," he answers. Then a car drives by, and Gonzo starts barking like a lunatic again.

"Listen," Nik says. "I should probably keep walking Gonzo. But, um, if you want, you can come with us. I mean, if your cousin is sleeping and all, and you want some company. I mean, I wouldn't mind the company. Because Gonzo, well, he's kind of nuts."

You smile at Nik and his invite. Then you look back at the house, where Tasha is asleep by the pool.

*Turn to page 103 if you agree to go
on a walk with Nik and Gonzo.*

- - - - -

*Turn to page 113 if you decide
to stay by the pool.*

YOU look out at the pool in the backyard. It's surrounded by a brick patio and tons of shrubs and flowers and one medium-tall fig tree. Your uncle Ted is very into figs. But what you don't see out there are boys. Not even half a boy. Not even a quarter.

"How about I wash my face and brush my hair and we head to the beach?" you say to Tasha.

She squeezes your shoulder. "I was hoping that's what you were going to say."

You put on your red polka-dot bikini, wash your face, reapply waterproof mascara, and brush your hair into a sleek ponytail. Then you walk over to Tasha's room with a tube of sunscreen in your hand.

"Can you help?" you ask her.

She nods, tying the final string of her bright yellow bikini. "Then you'll do me?"

"Sure," you say, handing over the lotion.

She slathers it all over your back and you do the same for her. Then you both make sure your arms and legs and stomachs and faces are covered.

"Don't forget your ears," Tasha says. "Or the tops of your feet. No one wants a flip-flop tan."

You think that you actually might like a flip-flop tan, but you follow her advice and rub some lotion on your feet, too.

Continue to page 197.

YOU take your bag to the changing room, put on your bathing suit, and grab a chaise lounge next to Tasha. Jade is on her other side, looking through her bag for something.

"So," Tasha says to you, "Jade and I need some help. What's your opinion on posters?"

"Posters?" you ask.

Tasha nods. "You know, things some people hang on their walls to decorate them."

Oh no. They've roped you into their dorm room decorating debate now, and you're not sure what the right answer is here. "I know what a poster is," you tell Tasha. "Is there an opinion to have about them? I mean, they're posters."

Tasha puts her hand to her heart as if you've mortally wounded her. "Are you sure we're related?" she asks.

"Found it!" Jade says, pulling a catalog from her bag. "This one has some great decorating ideas."

"What does our being related have to do with posters?" you ask Tasha, genuinely curious now.

"I hate them," Tasha says. "I think they're a sad imitation of art."

You never thought of a poster that way before, but, come to think of it, maybe she's right. . . .

"Of course they are," Jade says. "But it's not like we're going to bring your parents' Kandinsky with us to college. If you want art on the wall, it has to be posters. Otherwise, the place won't have any personality."

"What about photographs?" you offer. "Maybe you could do something with those? Frame them?"

"We're related after all!" Tasha says triumphantly. "That's just what I suggested!"

Jade rubs her forehead. "But how do we choose the photographs? And what if some of the people we end up posting pictures of turn into doinks in college and then we're stuck with framed pictures of them on our wall?"

Before Tasha can respond in what you're pretty certain is a rehash of a conversation they've had a million times already, you ask Jade something you've been wondering about since lunch. "What's a doink, exactly?"

Jade looks at you, at a loss for words. "I'm, um, it's a doink, you know? Just what it sounds like."

It doesn't really sound like much to you.

"It's, like, someone who's kind of nuts," Tasha says.

"Like someone who's nuts, but also kind of dorky," Jade clarifies. "A nutty dork is a doink."

"Got it," you tell them. You wonder how many other words they've created. And you wonder if they're all as lame as *doink*.

Jade opens up the catalog she found in her bag and spreads it out on Tasha's chair. There's a page showing bedding with a maroon, navy, and hunter green pattern on it. "What do you think?" she asks Tasha. "I thought maybe this would go with our color scheme. We can figure out wall hangings later."

Tasha starts to respond, and you stop paying attention. If they want your opinion again, you know they'll ask. Besides, there might be some cute boys up here at the pool for you to flirt with.

You check out the other chaise lounges, but most of the people on them look as if they're about your parents' age. There are a few kids, too. And maybe some grandparents. No one flirt-age-appropriate. You check out the two lifeguards on duty who are both very cute, but decide to pass because they seem to be eyeing each other and smiling when they're not watching the pool. You wouldn't be surprised if they were dating.

Then you spot him. A guy who looks to be about your age, wrangling a set of triplets and having a hard time of it. He's got his shirt off, and his abs are kind of incredible, but the killer abs don't seem to be helping him with the triplets.

"Come on, Sloanie," he's saying to the girl who's wrapped around his leg. "You love swimming lessons!"

"No, *I hate* them," she responds, sliding down so she's sitting on his foot, making it impossible for him to move.

"Remember how much fun you had last time?" he pleads. "You blew bubbles!"

"I blew bubbles, too," one of the boys says.

"And me," says the other boy.

"You totally did, guys," Abs tells them. "You were awesome. Just like Sloane."

"I was awesomer than Sloane," the first boy declares, "because she didn't put her head under."

"I put my head under for longer than you," the second boy tells the first.

You've done your fair share of neighborhood babysitting and can see this turning into a complete toddler meltdown in approximately ten seconds. You figure this guy can handle it, if he's been watching these kids for a while, but you wonder for a moment if you should offer to help. If you were in his situation, you would absolutely welcome some assistance, but it's hard to know about other people. Sometimes folks get a little touchy about help.

Turn to page 45 if you get up and offer him a hand.

- - - - -

Turn to page 187 if you decide he can handle it and you'd rather slather yourself in sunscreen than toddler tears.

"I'LL play," you say. "Is that okay, Tash? I'll meet up with you and Jade at the pool later?"

"Of course it's okay!" Tasha says, and wiggles her eyebrows. You realize that Tasha has very expressive eyebrows, and you're pretty sure you know what that wiggle means.

Since the valet guys know Dex, he doesn't have a ticket for his car, so he has to walk out with you to grab your stuff.

"We'll meet you on the courts," he tells the tennis group. "Which ones did you reserve?"

"Four and five," the guy you're beginning to think of as Head Tennis Guy says. "See you soon."

You follow Dex off the patio and down the steps to the parking lot. He waves at the valet guys. "I just need to grab her bag from my car," he tells them. "Could you give me the keys?"

One of the valets heads into a little hut that has keys hanging off nails on the wall, grabs Dex's set, and tosses them to him. "It's in the back right corner of the lot," he says.

You and Dex head back there. "So really," Dex says, "how good are you?"

You're actually a pretty decent tennis player— you did make varsity your sophomore year—but you shrug. "I'm okay," you say. "I can hold my own."

He pops the trunk of his car, and you rummage through your bag, pulling out sneakers, socks, a tennis skirt, a sports bra, and a white collared shirt and throwing them into your tote. You dig through your clothes a bit more and find your visor and a bikini and cover-up just in case you decide to go to the pool later, then you sling the strap of your racket case across your back, and say, "Okay, ready."

Dex eyes the model name emblazoned across your racket case. "That's a nice one," he says. "If you're playing with that racket . . . well . . . how is it that I've known you for ten summers and we've never played tennis together?"

You shrug. "You never asked?"

He grins. "Well, I'm glad I did this year. I have a feeling we're going to kick some butt on the court."

✳

AFTER you've changed, you meet Dex's friends on courts four and five and they all introduce themselves. You learn that you and Dex are going to be playing best two out of three against Head Tennis Guy, whose name turns out to be Mitch, and his twin sister, Mila. Then the winner of your match will play the winner of the doubles match on court five.

"You want to start up at the net or at the baseline?" Dex asks you.

"Up," you tell him. Your net game is strong, and you figure you should put your best foot forward here so the group won't regret asking you to join.

After a little warm-up, Dex serves for the first point in the game, and the twins can't even get their rackets on the ball.

"Nice shot!" you tell him. He's even better than you remember.

He smiles at you briefly, but then his face goes back to intense concentration mode. You know you should watch the court, but it's hard to take your eyes off him when he looks that way—his brow furrowed, his top teeth biting his bottom lip ever so slightly. You can't help but wonder what that lip would feel like pressed against yours. Then he tosses the ball high, stretches out his racket, and whacks the ball across the court. Another ace.

"No fair!" Mila says. "You're going to bagel us! If you guys win six games and we win zero, I'm so not going to be happy."

"Want me to slow it down?" Dex asks.

"Yes!" Mila says, just as Mitch says, "No!"

Mitch is looking at you as he says, "We can take it. We're tough." Then he grins. Is he flirting with you?

Mila glares at her brother. "Fine. We can take it."

Dex smiles and serves again. This time the ball is a little slower, but you're not sure if it's by design or if it just happened that way. Mitch gets his racket on the ball and slams it back. You reach out for a volley and punch the ball back over the net with a ton of backspin, stopping the ball's momentum so it hardly bounces. A perfect drop shot.

"Forty–love," Dex says. "Nice one."

You smile at him.

"I don't think these teams are fair," Mila says to Mitch. "They're both really good."

Mitch looks over at you, then back at his sister. "So are you saying you think we should swap partners?"

Turn to page 167 if you offer to switch partners and play with Mitch.

- - - - -

Turn to page 171 if you say no way and keep playing with Dex.

EVEN though the lifeguard is pretty hot and has secrets in his eyes, and even though he just rescued someone's dog from drowning, you're not quite sure if he's right for you. He seems like a bit of a Boy Scout, almost too responsible—more like a best-friend type than a boyfriend type.

Instead, you mound the sand underneath your towel into a decent-size pillow and lay your head back so you can read. You get so absorbed in the bug book that the noise of the beach disappears and it's just you and Kafka and Gregor Samsa out there on the blanket. A couple of chapters later you decide to flip over so you don't end up with one of those tans that's on only one half of your body.

You look around for Tasha, wishing she'd materialize so she could reapply the sunscreen to your back, but instead of Tasha you find a guy wearing retro glasses and reading *The Iliad* a few towels over. He's smiling at something going on in the book and has a dimple in his left cheek. You look down at *The Metamorphosis* and decide he would not share Tasha's view of appropriate beach books. In fact, you're pretty sure he would think it was cool you were reading Kafka at the beach. His book seems even more serious than yours.

You think about Tasha's challenge and wonder if this guy might be the one to flirt with. You look at the sunscreen on your blanket. Could he perhaps help you apply it? But that might be too much, right off the bat. Maybe you could talk about books first . . . or maybe it's better to stay where you are.

Turn to page 55 if you walk over to the guy reading The Iliad.

- - - - -

Turn to page 61 if you decide to sunscreen yourself the best you can and keep reading.

YOU figure that any guy who saved a dog's life is worth saying hello to. Especially when that dog saver was checking you out on his way back to his lifeguard chair and had secrets in his eyes.

You put *The Metamorphosis* back in your tote bag, make sure your bikini is covering everything it's supposed to, and head over to the lifeguard stand.

"Hey," you say, yelling a little so he can hear you. "That was pretty impressive lifesaving."

The guard looks down from his chair and smiles at you. "Thanks," he says. Then his eyes dart back out over the water. "I have to monitor the swimmers, but if you want to climb up here, I can chat while I look. And you can be an extra pair of eyes."

You've actually always wondered what the beach

looks like from the top of a lifeguard chair, so you say sure.

"Just climb up the front," he says. "It's built like a ladder, for easy on and off."

"Aye aye, Captain," you say.

He laughs, still looking out at the ocean. "I'm not a sailor. Well, at least not at the moment."

When you get to the top of the stand, he shifts to the right to give you some room. You sit next to him and look out at the ocean.

"I'm J.R., by the way," he says.

You introduce yourself to him and then say, "What did you mean about not being a captain at the moment?" You're looking at his face in profile. It's a nice one. Smooth skin, shaved head, curling eyelashes, pouty lips.

"Oh, nothing really," he responds, focused on the water. "Just my older brother has a sailboat, and sometimes I sail with him. He always lets me captain the ship when I do."

That's one of the sweetest big-brother things you've ever heard. It makes you wish you had a big brother with a sailboat, even though you don't know how to sail.

"That's nice of him," you answer.

"Yeah, he's kind of like a dad to me," J.R. says.

You want to ask more about that, about what that means and why his brother has to act like a father, but it's the first conversation you've ever had with this guy, and you don't want to seem too pushy.

Luckily, J.R. continues without your prodding. "Our dad died when I was six and Chris was sixteen, and ever since then, he's taken care of me."

You think about that and about how J.R. is kind of taking care of the whole beach right now. How he took care of that dog. "So you pay it forward?" you ask.

He takes his gaze away from the beachfront for a second to look at you quizzically. "What do you mean?"

"The taking-care thing," you say. "Isn't that your job? To take care of people?"

"Huh," he says. "I never thought of that. Are you a psych major or something?"

"A high schooler," you answer. "Rising junior. What about you?"

"I just graduated from high school last month. I'm taking a gap year. Gonna work at my brother's boat dealership while I figure out what I want to do. Maybe be an EMT. That's top on my list now."

"EMT's cool," you say. "More taking care."

He laughs. "You're right."

Both of you are looking out at the water. In one section there are two people in kayaks and about ten people on surfboards, then in another section there are maybe double that number of kids on boogie boards and a handful of people swimming and jumping in the waves—one of them is probably Tasha, you think, but you can't tell which. There are also six people hanging on to the floating dock that's about seventy-five feet out into the ocean. Actually, maybe Tasha's there. It looks as if there's someone in bright yellow, but then again, it's possible there's another girl on this beach who owns a yellow suit. You have no idea how J.R.—and the other lifeguards who are down closer to the shore at the moment—can watch all of this at once.

You look over and see his eyes zipping back and forth, from right to left, left to right, scanning the water. His head is moving a little bit, too. You look out again and watch one of the kayakers. You've never kayaked before, but you think it looks like something that might be fun to try. Maybe Tasha knows where you can rent a kayak. Maybe tomorrow.

While you're watching, the kayaker gets caught

in a big wave and gets pushed pretty close to the jetty. He starts paddling away, but then you see a big wave heading straight toward him. You can't help but gasp. "Oh no! Watch out!" you cry, even though there's no way the kayaker can hear you. But J.R. can.

"What?" he asks, alarmed. "What is it?"

"The wave! The kayak!" You point toward the jetty.

"Oh hell!" he says, and blows his whistle, standing up on the chair's footrest. The people in the water turn to look at him, making sure they haven't gone out too far or anything, but the kayaker seems not to hear.

You watch in horror as the wave throws the kayak against the jetty and the tiny boat capsizes. Before you can register what happened, J.R. is off the chair with his rescue tube and running to the water. He dives in and swims in a perfect, superfast crawl stroke to where the boat capsized. By the time he gets there, the kayaker has popped up and is hanging on to his boat to stay afloat. You can't tell exactly what's going on from so away, but it looks as if maybe the guy's head is bleeding.

J.R. does some sort of maneuver that seems to stabilize the guy's head and neck and swims with him back to shore. He comes running back and grabs a backboard, while radioing some other guards and asking you to call 911.

You jump down from the chair and grab your phone. You've never made a 911 call, but you tell them what happened and that the lifeguard said to call, and they say an ambulance will be there as soon as possible.

Tasha comes out of the ocean and finds you on your towel, where you're standing and watching all this unfold. J.R. has the guy strapped onto a backboard so that his head and neck are immobilized, and two other lifeguards have come over from somewhere—maybe farther down on the beach? Other than the blood on his head, the guy seems mostly okay. He's alert and breathing and moving at least, and seems to be talking to some of the people gathered around him.

"What's going on?" Tasha asks, drying herself off.

"The guy's kayak got slammed into the jetty. It was really scary."

"You saw it?" Tasha asks, shaking her head to get water out of her ear.

"Yeah." You nod. "I was kind of flirting with the lifeguard, so I was up with him in his chair."

Tasha does her eyebrow raise, and you smile a little.

"But that's not important now," you say. "This guy could be really hurt!"

Sirens blaring, the ambulance pulls up to the edge of the parking lot. You go running and point out where the EMTs need to go. They get to the injured kayaker and talk to J.R. He nods a few times, and then helps them carry the guy on the backboard across the beach and load him onto a gurney waiting in the ambulance. Then J.R. and one of the other lifeguards head back over toward your towel and the chair.

When they get to you, J.R. stops.

"Is he going to be okay?" you ask.

J.R. nods. "I think so. The backboard was just a precaution because of his head injury. But he seemed okay when he left."

"I'm going to head up into the chair," the other lifeguard says. And J.R. nods at him.

"Sounds good," he says. "Glad you were here to help with that."

"No problem, man," Lifeguard Number Two says. He's already up and doing the ocean-scanning thing you saw J.R. doing earlier.

J.R. turns back to you. "So my shift's over. Any chance you want to walk with me and get ice cream or something? I think I need to decompress a little after that."

You look over at Tasha. She gives you a go-with-him! face.

But you're not sure what to do.

Turn to page 65 if you decide to take him up on his ice cream offer.

- - - - -

Turn to page 191 if you decide to say no thanks.

THE little girl wrapped around the guy's ankle starts to cry, and he bends down to pick her up.

"No swimming, no swimming, no swimming," she says over and over.

He sits down with her on the edge of a chaise lounge and tells the boys to sit next to him. They don't. One picks up a towel and wears it as a cape.

"I am Super Monster Blake Man, and I'm going to eat you!" he shouts to his brother and starts to lumber after him, heading toward the bathroom.

The boy without the cape takes one running step forward, clearly trying to get ahead of his brother, and one of the lifeguards blows his whistle.

"No running on the pool deck!" the lifeguard yells from his chair.

Now it looks as if the no-cape brother is about to cry as well.

"Come here, Leo," Mr. Killer Abs says, with his arms still full of Sloane, who seems to have stopped crying.

Leo doesn't come, though; he seems frozen in place.

"Blake, you, too," Killer Abs says.

But Blake is too busy being Super Monster Blake Man and karate kicking invisible enemies. You take pity on Killer Abs and get up off your chaise lounge.

"Hey," you say as you get closer, "you need any help?"

Abs looks up at you for a minute as if he's going to say no, but then lets out a breath. "If you know how to get this one to like swimming lessons or those two to listen to directions, be my guest."

You look at Sloane and then you look at the boys. "Let me try to talk to her," you say. "You can deal with the Super Monster and statue man over there."

Sloane is still hugging his neck, not letting go, so you start up a conversation.

"Hi," you say to Sloane.

"Hi," she says back.

"I like your bathing suit." She has a red one with ruffles all along the edges. Luckily, you're wearing a red bathing suit, too. "It's the same color as mine," you point out to her.

She looks at your bikini; it's red with white polka dots.

"I don't have spots," she tells you.

"Boys!" Killer Abs says. "Come here!"

The boys don't listen.

"Do you like my spots?" you ask Sloane.

She nods, and then unlocks her hands from around Killer Abs's neck. "I have a mermaid on my tummy," she tells you. "Look."

"That's beautiful!" you say. "Can I see it up close?"

She climbs off Killer Abs's lap and stands in front of you. He mouths the words *thank you*, then gets up and zooms over to Leo and Blake while you and Sloane continue to chat about mermaids and how mermaids all take swimming lessons.

By the time Killer Abs has returned with Leo and Blake, Sloane is very excited about being a mermaid and learning to swim.

"Nice work," Killer Abs says, nodding at you. "I could've used your help all morning. I'm Adam, by the way."

You introduce yourself to him. "Nice to meet you," you tell him.

"Likewise," he answers.

Three swim instructors are heading your way, after dropping kids off at their parents' lounge chairs.

"Private swim lessons," Adam tells you. "One instructor for each. Too bad it's not private babysitters, too."

"You'll be here in half an hour?" one of the instructors asks Adam.

"Absolutely," Adam says. "And you have my cell if something happens before then. If I leave the pool area, I won't go far."

The triplets all say good-bye and head off for their swim lessons, Sloane telling her instructor how she wants to learn to swim like a mermaid.

Adam turns to you. "Thank you," he says. "Seriously. Thank you. Sloane had a bad morning. And the boys freak when I pay more attention to her than I do to them."

"No problem," you tell him. "Is it really just you and the three of them all day?"

"Pretty much," he tells you, running his hand through his straight, jet-black hair. It's longer in the front than it is in the back. "But their parents pay a lot."

You laugh. "Well, seems like you're earning it."

He sighs. "Yeah," he says. "Listen, I was going to go over to the snack bar and grab a soda or something. Maybe take a little walk around. Any chance you want to join me? It's the least I can do to thank you for your assistance back there."

If you decide to hang with Adam,
go to page 71.

- - - - -

If you've had your fill of Adam and
the triplets and would rather go back
to Jade and Tasha, go to page 51.

"THAT'S such a nice offer," you say to Adam. "But it's my first day here, and I've been planning on some major relaxation time."

He flicks some hair out of his eyes. "And there's nothing I can do to change your mind?"

He *is* pretty cute, but you think about the chatting and the flirting and the thinking about what you say and making sure you're being witty and clever and fun, and you just don't think you can handle it right now.

"Not today," you tell him. "But really, thank you for asking."

Adam nods his head and says, "Well, it was still nice to meet you. And thanks again. I hope the kids behave during their swim lessons and don't interrupt your relaxing time."

You laugh. "Don't worry," you tell him. "I've got headphones, and I'm not afraid to use 'em."

"You may need to blast your music if one of those guys gets to wailing."

"Duly noted," you tell Adam. "Enjoy your break."

He looks as if he's about to say something more, but instead salutes you, which is kind of goofy, but somehow kind of cute, too. And it makes you wonder if maybe he's going into the military or something. Especially with those abs.

> *You salute him back and*
> *head over to your chair.*
> *Continue to page 187.*

YOU look back and forth between the two guys. Dex's blond curls are flopping in the breeze, and his cheekbones look especially chiseled in the sun. His eyes are soft and pleading.

"I think I'll give Dex a chance to apologize," you say.

Mitch looks disappointed, but Dex's grin has turned into a full-fledged smile. "I promise I'll make my apology worth your while," he says, holding his hand out to you.

As you walk, he starts to apologize in earnest. "The twins can be . . . a lot sometimes. And Mitch is so competitive. I just try to go with whatever they want and not get into it with them. I'm sorry if I made you feel like I didn't want to play with you. That couldn't be further from the truth."

He looks at you with his navy blue eyes. "Do you forgive me?" he asks.

You look at him sideways. "I'm thinking about it," you tell him.

Turn to page 193.

YOU'VE always had a thing for smart guys—even back in kindergarten you had a crush on the one boy who could already read, Danny Jung. He left after kindergarten, moved to another state, you heard. You wonder for a brief minute what happened to him and vow to Google him later. He used to have a lunchbox that looked like a barn. A red one. With horses and pigs painted on it. That's another reason you liked him back then. Yours was just plain with stripes.

Anyway, this particular smart guy, the one on the beach now reading *The Iliad*, seems as if he's worth a try. You take your book in one hand and the sunscreen in the other and walk over to his towel.

"Hi," you say. "I'm sorry to interrupt you, but I just wanted to tell you that I like your taste in books." You show him the spine on yours. There's a little Penguin on it, matching the one on his. "I think our books are related."

He looks up at you with eyes the color of olives and laughs. "Definitely cousins." Then he turns his sideways so you can see how thick it is. "Mine's the overweight cousin. The one everyone talks about behind his back when he helps himself to a fourth hamburger and a fifth slice of blueberry pie."

You turn your book sideways. "I think mine's the cousin who probably could use a second burger and goes to Zumba classes every morning."

"Zumba?" he asks.

You shake your head. "Never mind. Some sort of dance workout thing my mom does."

He nods sagely. "Zumba. Got it." Then he notices the tube of sunscreen in your hand. "Do you always carry sunscreen when you compliment people's books?"

This is your opening! "Well," you say, "not always. But I'm having a sunscreen emergency right now, and, actually, I was wondering if you could help."

"A sunscreen emergency?" he asks, his eyes getting wider. "That sounds serious."

You nod and put on your most serious face. "Oh, it is," you tell him. "Incredibly serious. If someone doesn't put sunscreen on my back right now, I might turn into a lobster."

His eyes go to your book. "Better than an insect," he says. "Or what's the actual description? A monstrous vermin?"

You flip open *The Metamorphosis*. He's quoted it exactly. "How'd you know that?" you ask.

He shrugs. "Words stick in my head. Read that one last year. I'm Marco, by the way."

You introduce yourself and ask, "Did you read it for class?"

He nods, then holds up *The Iliad* again, this time with the cover facing you. "This one's summer reading for college. But it's pretty good."

You're shocked. "College gives you homework over the summer?"

He sighs. "Yeah. Columbia does, at least. All incoming first years have to read this one. It seems right to read it on the beach, though, because of lines like: 'He saileth in his many-benched ship over the wine-dark sea.'"

You look out at the ocean. "Doesn't look so 'wine-dark' to me," you say.

Marco laughs. "Good point. So you want me to sunscreen you up?"

You hand over the tube of sunscreen, and he pats the blanket in front of him. You sit down.

"I heard you're supposed to use about a shot glass full of sunscreen per application," he says. "But since this is just for your back . . . what do you think, a quarter of a shot glass?"

You twist your neck around to see if he's serious about this. You can't really tell. "A quarter of a shot glass sounds good to me," you say.

He nods and starts squeezing sunscreen into his palm. "I think that's about right," he says, holding his hand out so you can see it.

"Looks good," you say, trying not to laugh. There's something kind of endearing about how seriously he's taking this sunscreen job.

He rubs the sunscreen into your back, and you feel how strong his fingers are. You wonder if he does finger exercises to strengthen them. Do people make finger weights? Little finger barbells? Or maybe it's from the piano or something.

"Do you play an instrument?" you ask.

His hands disappear from your back. "I do," he says. "The guitar. Why do you ask?"

You're glad he's facing your back, because you know you're blushing. "You, um, have really strong fingers," you say.

He rubs more sunscreen across your shoulders and the back of your neck. "I've got calluses, too, though, so they're not very soft. Guitar strings are not kind to fingertips."

His hands disappear from your back again. "You're all rubbed in," he says.

You flip around on the towel so you're facing him. "Thanks," you say. "I really appreciate it. I should probably let you get back to your book now."

Marco looks at you for a long moment. "You could," he says. "Or you could take a walk with me along the shoreline. I think I might need a break from *The Iliad*, as lovely as it is."

You're intrigued. You know that if you tell this

story to Tasha, it'll totally count as a point in the flirting challenge. But you wonder if Marco could be a point in the kissing challenge, too.

Turn to page 77 if you want to go for a walk with Marco.

- - - - -

Turn to page 209 if you realize Tasha's been gone a while and think you should probably go find her.

AS cute as retro-glasses guy and his dimple are, you decide you'd rather keep reading your book. You sunscreen your back as best you can and flip over onto your stomach. But before you have a chance to get too involved in your book, a Frisbee comes sailing out of nowhere and conks you in the back of your head.

"Ow!" you say out loud to no one in particular.

You sit up and rub the spot where the Frisbee collided with your skull. It's not the first time you've been hit in the head with a Frisbee—your neighbor from home is part of an Ultimate team, and has convinced you to play a few times—but it's never pleasant when it happens.

"You okay?" you hear the lifeguard shout down to you.

You look up at him. "I think so," you shout back.

"You want me to take a look at it?" he asks, still in his spot on the guard stand.

"I think I'll be all right," you answer.

Then you hear someone shouting at you from farther down the beach. "Hey! Chick in the red bathing suit! Can you toss that disc back?"

"You just hit me with this thing!" you yell, picking up the Frisbee and standing next to your towel.

"I'm so sorry! It got caught in the wind," the guy answers. "Can you throw it back?"

With a smirk, you toss the Frisbee so it lands halfway between your towel and the place he's standing, right on top of a garbage pail.

"Sorry!" you yell back. "It must've gotten caught in the wind."

You hear someone chuckling and look up. It's the lifeguard. "Nice one," he says, when he sees you facing him.

You find yourself laughing, too. And wondering if maybe flirting with a nice Boy Scout–type could be a good thing after all. But before you can make your decision, Frisbee Guy comes over, having retrieved his Frisbee.

"I want to apologize," he says, "and compliment

your arm. Not just anyone can pitch a disc onto a trash can like that."

You smile and feel yourself blushing. He totally knew that you threw the Frisbee onto the garbage pail on purpose. "Sorry about that," you say.

He smiles back. "I'll forgive you," he says, "if you agree to play with us. It's co-ed, and we need a girl— especially one with an arm like that."

You thank him for the offer, but you're not completely sure if you want to play. Plus, Tasha's been gone for a while. And there's the lifeguard you shared that moment with before, who saved a dog's life and seems like he might be much more interesting than he first appeared.

As Frisbee Guy starts to walk away, you're still not certain what to do next.

*Turn to page 37 if you get up
and talk to the lifeguard.*

- - - - -

*Turn to page 83 if you decide to
go looking for Tasha.*

- - - - -

*Turn to page 213 if you decide
to play Frisbee.*

THINKING about it a little more, you decide that ice cream with J.R. actually might be the perfect cure for seeing someone almost drown.

"Sure," you say. "Ice cream sounds great."

"Let me just grab my shirt and wallet," he says. He jogs over to the lifeguard stand and pulls a red duffel bag out from underneath it. When he slips on his T-shirt, you're a little disappointed. Muscles like his should never be hidden under clothing. You throw on your cover-up and a pair of flip-flops, and then J.R.'s back and walking with you over to the ice cream stand.

"What a crazy day," he says.

"That sort of thing doesn't usually happen?" you ask.

J.R. shakes his head. "Not at all. Like, maybe

ten times all summer. This is a private beach, so it's pretty small. Not a ton of people means not a ton of problems, usually. But today, I don't know. Maybe it's a full moon or something."

You wonder if it is. And if that sort of thing really makes a difference.

"Do you believe in magic?" you ask him.

"Magic?" he asks.

"You know, the full moon affecting people." You're asking because of that, but also because somehow, you're feeling drawn to J.R. Almost magically. You're not sure if it's because you watched him save someone's life, or because of his underwear-ad-campaign-ready body, or because he actually seems like a really nice guy, but there's magnetism there.

"Oh," he says, and then stays quiet for a moment. "I believe in the possibility of magic."

You nod. "I like that. I think I believe in the possibility of magic, too."

You've made it to the ice cream stand, and you look at all of the options written on the chalkboard wall.

"What would you like?" J.R. asks. "My treat, because you spotted that guy first."

"Oh, you don't have to!" you say.

"I know." He reaches into his bathing suit pocket for his wallet. "I'm not doing it because I have to. I want to."

That magical magnetism feels as if it just ratcheted up a notch, and you can't quite look away from J.R.

"Double chocolate chip with chocolate sprinkles," you say. "In a wafer cone."

That's your favorite ice cream combo and has been forever.

J.R. smirks.

"What's so funny?" you ask.

"I was planning to get vanilla with rainbow sprinkles in a cup."

"Opposites attract?" you ask out loud, before you realize the words have made it from your brain to your mouth.

But thankfully, J.R. smiles. "Opposites attract," he says.

J.R. pays, and you take your ice creams over to a bench. You lick your cone quietly, feeling the stress and panic of the near-drowning situation leaving your body. You look over at J.R., wondering if he's feeling the same thing.

He's already looking at you. "I liked what you

noticed about me before. About me taking care of people. That . . . it meant a lot somehow."

You shrug. "It seemed obvious," you say as you lick your cone again.

"Not to everyone," J.R. says. "Not everyone listens like that. Or bothers to notice."

You move your cone up and run your tongue around the edge to catch all the drips before they make it down to your hand. Then you say, "People must be nuts not to listen to you. Or notice you."

J.R.'s quiet for a minute. "You have some ice cream on your lip," he says.

You're horrified. It must be pretty disastrous if he bothered to say something to you about it. "Where?" you ask, swiping at your mouth.

"Let me," he says.

You tip your face toward him, and the next thing you know his lips are on yours. You're surprised for a second, and then he slowly pulls away.

"All clean," he says, looking down at his ice cream. He eats a spoonful. You wonder if maybe he's embarrassed. You wonder if you should say, "That was nice" or "Thank you" or something, but those both seem lame.

"J.R.?" you finally say.

He looks back at you.

"I think you have some ice cream on your lip, too."

This time, you lean toward him, and this time you're not surprised, and this time the kiss lasts so long you start to feel short of breath.

You pull away and then scoot closer to J.R. on the bench. He puts his arm around your shoulder and hugs you in closer to him. You lean your head against his chest, and he rests his chin on your hair, tucking you tight against him. And you decide that this moment—right here, right now—is exactly the birthday present you'd be hoping to get this weekend. And it makes you believe that the existence of magic is more than just a possibility.

CONGRATULATIONS!
YOU'VE FOUND YOUR HAPPY ENDING!

YOU look over at Tasha and Jade. They're pointing to different pages in the catalog and seem to be arguing. You look back at Adam.

"Sure," you say. "A soda sounds great. A walk, too."

The two of you head toward the snack bar, and you can't help but notice how tall Adam is. It seems as if he could tuck your head right underneath his chin. Actually, you might need a pair of heels to reach his chin.

"Are you six five?" you blurt out. "Six four?"

"Six three," he tells you, with a smile. "And yes, I do play basketball."

That might explain the abs. He's clearly an athlete.

"So where are the triplets' parents?" you ask him.

You're at the snack bar now. He orders himself a Sprite and asks what you want. "Orange soda," you tell him.

"Huh," he says before ordering your drink. "I had you pegged for a Diet Coke. That's what most of the girls here drink." He signs the chit for both drinks and hands you yours.

"I guess I'm not like most of the girls," you say. You're definitely flirting now.

He looks intrigued. "I guess not. Anyway, their dad is golfing, and their mom is playing tennis. Then she's getting a manicure and having her hair done for some party they're going to tonight."

You nod and take a sip of your soda. The orangey tang explodes in your mouth. You can't understand why everyone doesn't drink orange soda. It's clearly the best soda ever invented.

"And how did you end up working for them?"

Adam takes a gulp of his Sprite. "My sister did it last year, but she's spending the summer in France as an au pair for a family over there. So she handed the gig over to me. We have two little half sisters—five and six now—so I've got little-kid experience, but these three are a lot."

"Yeah, you totally have your hands full," you say.

While you were talking, Adam steered you toward the dock, where the country club members tie up their boats. Tasha's parents don't have one, but you see Jade and Dex's dad's sailboat bobbing in the water. It's called *The Lady Eileen*, named after Jade and Dex's mom.

"But like I said before, the pay's great." Adam sits down on the dock and slips off his flip-flops. He dangles his feet in the water. "I'm saving up for a car, and I think I'll make enough this summer to get the one I want."

You wonder how great the pay really is. And think about the fact that Adam's saving up to buy a car himself. When Tasha turned seventeen, her parents bought her a car, and your parents said they'd do the same for you next year.

"What are you looking to get?" you ask, sitting down next to him.

"Want to guess?" He leans back on his elbows, and now his head is about level with yours.

You think about the facts you've learned. Athletic, hard worker, big family . . .

"A Jeep?" you ask.

He laughs, a rumbly one, deep in his stomach. "The exact opposite. I want a two-seater convertible.

A 1986 Corvette. It's the car my dad had in college, and he always used to talk about how awesome it was. Plus, if it's small, I won't get roped into doing too much little-sister chauffeuring."

You could see him in an old-school Corvette. It works. Maybe better than a Jeep.

"So now you just have to make it through a summer with the triplets." You lean back on your elbows, too, so your shoulder is next to his arm. Adam is so different from the guys you know. He seems more real, somehow. More grown-up, even though he must be about the same age as Dex.

"Oh, I'll make it through," he says. "Especially if you're around to give me a hand."

You give him a sad smile. "I won't be," you say. "I'm only visiting for the weekend. My cousin's here all summer, but I'm going home on Sunday night."

He takes another sip of soda. "Well, that's too bad," he says. "You're the nicest girl I've run into at this country club."

He slides his flip-flops back on and stands up, then reaches out a hand to help you to your feet. Well, that was fast.

"I can get up myself," you tell him, as you slip your own flip-flops back on.

"Of course you can," he answers, "but I'm being a gentleman."

Would a gentleman cut off a conversation just because the person he's talking to won't be there the whole summer long? But still, you smile and reach for his hand. He's incredibly strong and pulls you up off the ground so quickly you lose your balance and start to fall. "Maybe I can't do it myself," you say, as he catches you and stops you from tipping into the water.

You're wrapped in his arms and pressed against his killer abs, your head right under his collarbone. You tilt your head back and look up at him. "Happy to catch you," he says.

You think for a moment that he might kiss you. A crazy thought, an impossible thought, but once it enters your head, you decide you might like for that kiss to happen. You lock eyes, but instead of kissing you on the lips, Adam dips his head down and plants a kiss on your forehead. Somehow it feels almost as romantic. Maybe even more so. There's something sweet about being kissed on the forehead, and you realize that no guy you've ever been with has ever done that to you before.

He sighs and looks at you like he's struggling with some sort of internal decision.

"Are you free later?" he asks, after about thirty seconds of inner struggling. "Can I take you out properly? To dinner? To the jazz festival on the beach?"

Turn to page 183 if you want to go out with Adam later.

- - - - -

Turn to page 185 if you'd rather not.

"IS that an invitation?" you ask.

"Why, I believe it is," Marco says, standing up.

He holds out his hands and helps you to your feet. Adorable, dimpled, smart, and a gentleman! Though now you're wondering if he might not exactly be the type to kiss a girl he's just met.

"Is that an answer?" he asks.

You nod. "It is. I would love to go for a walk along the shoreline with you. Let me just text my cousin so she knows where I am when she gets back to the towels."

You walk over to your bag, grab your phone, and text Tasha:

Working on your flirting challenge.

Be back soon.

Then Marco crooks his elbow and says, "May I escort you to the ocean?"

You bite your lip to keep from laughing and hook your elbow around his. "Of course you may," you answer. You can see that Marco is fighting laughter, too.

"So," you say, as the two of you make your way to the water's edge, "do you know what you're going to major in at college?"

"At Columbia you can't really declare until second semester sophomore year," he says. "But I'm pretty sure I want to be a philosophy major."

"Why philosophy?" you ask.

You're not even exactly sure what you study when you're a philosophy major. You have a feeling it involves reading a lot of books by old Greek people, maybe old French people, too. Or maybe you're totally off.

"Well, philosophy, if you dissect the word," Marco says, "means love of wisdom. I like the idea of debating the big questions, looking for the wisdom in sweeping ideas like truth and beauty and knowledge and reason."

You reach far back into your brain for a line of poetry your English teacher had written on a banner above the whiteboard. "Like, 'Beauty is truth, truth beauty'?" you ask.

"'That is all ye know on earth, and all ye need

know,'" Marco finishes for you. "Keats. 'Ode on a Grecian Urn.' The enigmatic ending. That's probably more an English major thing to study, but the connection between truth and beauty is interesting to debate. There could definitely be a philosophical discussion about that."

"The truth is sometimes ugly," you say, thinking about doctors having to tell people that they're dying, teachers having to tell parents that there's something wrong with their kids.

"But can there be beauty in ugliness?" Marco asks. "People still find beauty during wartime."

Your brain is working overtime to keep up with Marco, but you like it. It's the most interesting conversation you've had maybe ever.

"Aren't beauty and ugliness opposites, though?" you ask. "How can you find something in its opposite?"

You've turned and are walking parallel to the water, the waves lapping cold against your toes.

"This guy I know," Marco says, "photographs rust-covered Dumpsters and corroded pipes, but he zooms in really tight, so you can't tell what you're looking at. And it's kind of gorgeous. It looks like modern art, all color and emotion."

"So you're saying ugly can be beautiful." You look over at him.

"And beautiful can be ugly," he says. "But sometimes, beautiful is just beautiful and ugly is just ugly."

You laugh. "Nothing is everything, but sometimes everything is everything and nothing is nothing."

"Pretty much." His dimple is back, and you fight the urge to poke your finger into it.

"Did you have a final destination in mind?" you ask him.

He points to the rocks about a dozen feet in front of you. "The jetty," he says.

"I used to climb on those rocks with my cousin," you tell him.

"I did, too—well, not with my cousin. Or your cousin. By myself," he answers. "Maybe we used to see each other."

You try to remember seeing a smaller, younger version of Marco on the rocks, but you can't. "I wasn't here that often," you say. "Usually just for a few days each summer."

You've made it to the jetty, and Marco starts to climb. You follow, until you're both balancing on top of the closest rock.

"How daring are you?" he asks.

The truth is usually you're not very daring at all, but something's different now. You decide to be as daring as Marco wants you to be.

"Very," you answer.

His dimple comes back for another visit, and he steps from your rock to the one in front. "Follow me then."

You do, and carefully put your feet wherever he's put his, as you move farther and farther out into the ocean, balancing on the slippery black boulders. When you've reached the farthest point on the jetty, Marco stops. You stop next to him.

"This is my favorite spot on the whole beach," he says. "The waves, the wind, the height up here. It's beautiful beautiful, not ugly beautiful."

He closes his eyes and tips his face up toward the sun. You close your eyes, too, and feel your hair whipping behind you in the wind.

"You look beautiful beautiful, too," Marco says. "Like you could command the ocean. Like you're its queen."

You open your eyes and look at him. His face looks so open that you can tell it's not a line. He's being honest. What was that about truth and beauty again?

Something in you melts a little.

"If I'm a queen," you say, "I think that means I need a king. You interested in the job?"

Marco slides his arm over your shoulder. "It would be an honor," he says. You lean your head against his and look out at the ocean. A queen with her king, ready to command the waves.

Even without a kiss, this moment is perfect, and you wouldn't trade it for anything.

CONGRATULATIONS!
YOU'VE FOUND YOUR HAPPY ENDING!

YOU wave good-bye to Frisbee Guy, and even though the lifeguard makes you wonder if perhaps Boy Scouts could make good boyfriends after all, you decide you'd probably turn him off pretty quickly with your un–Girl Scout ways, and you would rather spare yourself the rejection. Also, you realize that Tasha has been gone for a big chunk of the afternoon. You decide to go look for her. But just as you start to scan the ocean for her bright yellow bikini, you see her walking out of the ocean, making a beeline for you and the towels.

Continue to page 205.

YOU get to the house, jump out of the car, and grab your bag from the trunk.

"Yellow room or blue room?" Tasha asks you. Her parents' house has four bedrooms: the master, which is off limits, Tasha's room, and two guest rooms.

"Yellow," you say. "I want the king bed."

"Of course you do." Tasha wiggles her eyebrows at you.

You ignore her and walk into the house. The downstairs, which is one of those huge rooms that is part kitchen, part dining room, and part living room, looks pretty much the same as it did last summer, with its distressed wood furniture, blue and gray accents, seascapes hanging on the walls, and huge windows looking out over the deck and the pool.

"Lemonade?" Tasha asks. "My mom said she

ordered the summer essentials for us, and Linda the House Sitter unpacked them."

"Oh, that was nice," you say, dropping your bag on the floor and heading into the kitchen area. "I'll get us some." Once you fill two glasses, you stop under the skylight and look up at the blue, cloudless sky. Tasha comes to stand next to you and takes her lemonade.

"Gorgeous, huh?" she asks, after she swallows her first sip.

"Gorgeous," you repeat.

"Just like us," Tasha says, throwing her arm across your shoulder and laughing.

You smile and give her a little shove. "You are so ridiculous!" you tell her.

"Perhaps," she answers, draining the rest of her glass. "So, are we going to be gorgeous here by the pool, or would you rather be gorgeous at the beach?"

*Turn to page 15 if you decide
to be gorgeous by the pool.*

- - - - -

*Turn to page 21 if you decide
to be gorgeous at the beach.*

INSTEAD of waving back to the second fisherman, you turn to Tasha and say, "What would you think about heading home?"

"No cute fisherman?" she asks.

You shake your head. "I think I'd rather have some lemonade and a dip in the pool."

"That does sound pretty good," Tasha answers.

The two of you get up, toss the trash from your lobster rolls, and go back to where you left your towels so you can pick up all your stuff from the beach. Then you head back to Tasha's house.

Once you get there, Tasha says, "So we're gonna be gorgeous by the pool?"

"Gorgeous by the pool," you say. "At least for now."

Continue to page 15.

THERE are only a couple more people who have to order before you and Tasha.

"Are you getting something?" Tasha asks. "I think I want the No Frills."

You look at the menu. The No Frills is just lobster and mayo on a toasted hot-dog bun.

You weren't feeling that hungry when you started the trip over to the food trucks, but now with the smell of toasting bread and lobster, you're starting to change your mind. You read the rest of the options. There's the Hot Stuff, which involves chili powder. You're not so much interested in that. There's the Garden Variety, which has some lettuce and celery and cabbage worked in there. You figure that'll probably just dilute the flavor of lobster. Then there's Drawn and Quartered—chunks of lobster, drawn butter, a toasted bun, and a squeeze of lemon. That looks pretty good to you. And it has been a while since you ate.

"I'm going for the Drawn and Quartered," you say.

"Mmm," Tasha answers. "Then your lips will be all salty for when you kiss the lobster-roll guy."

"Tash!" you say.

The two people in front of you get their lobster rolls, and you and Tasha step forward. You're in front of the ordering window now, and the lobster-roll guy leans out his little window.

He smiles at you, and his grin takes over his face. It looks like the kind that could be in a toothpaste commercial.

"I was waiting for you to get to the head of the line," he says. "What can I get for you?"

You swallow. You can't believe he noticed you—like, really noticed you, out of all of the people in line.

"Um," you say.

Tasha gently nudges you.

You clear you throat and smile. You need to get it together here!

"One Drawn and Quartered for me, and a No Frills for my cousin," you say, indicating Tasha. Then you add, "please."

"Pretty and polite!" Lobster Roll Guy says. He winks at you as he prepares your order.

"Oh, she's more than that," Tasha tells him.

Lobster Roll Guy smiles again, but this time he only uses half of his mouth, not his whole toothpaste grin. "I bet she is."

Then he turns to you. "What are your favorite chips?" he asks.

Chips? You look at the display of potato chips running along one side of his food truck.

"Salt and vinegar," you say, "but I don't need any chips."

"Those are my favorite, too!" he says, as he hands you Tasha's roll. You pass it over to her and wonder if he would've said that no matter what you'd answered.

"What about you?" he asks Tasha.

"Jalapeño," she answers.

"Spicy," he replies, handing you your own roll.

"Don't you know it," Tasha says, taking a bite of hers. "Mmm, this is delicious."

You and Tasha pay, and Tasha says, "Want to go eat these by the wharf?"

You do, but you also want to keep talking to Lobster Roll Guy.

"There's a great bench that's kind of hidden by

the enormous trawler at the edge of the pier," he tells you, as he hands you two bags of potato chips—one salt and vinegar and one jalapeño. "These are on the house."

"Thank you!" you say. You were kind of hoping he'd invite you to . . . well . . . to do something. But since he hasn't, you wonder if you should invite him. He has made it kind of clear that he likes you . . . at least, you think he has.

Turn to page 119 if you invite him to meet up with you after he gets off work.

- - - - -

Turn to page 123 if you don't say anything more and go to watch the fishermen unload their catch at the wharf.

"**SO,**" Tasha says. "Lobsterman or Surfman? Jean Paul sounds sexy. I think you should try it out."

"And leave Lobsterman to you?" you tease.

"We'll see," she says. "But this weekend is about you! Your birthday, your kiss—excuse me, your flirt-and-maybe-a-kiss-if-you-feel-like-it."

You nod your head. "I'm glad you got it right this time."

You think about it. It could be cool to learn to surf. But you're not so sure how good you'd be.

"What if I stink at it?" you ask Tasha.

"So you'll need some extra help. That means more time with sexy Jean Paul."

You consider that.

"What if he's, like, forty?" you ask. "And gross?"

"Then you chalk it up to taking a chance, and

you'll see if you like surfing. And if that happens, I promise we'll find a party somewhere tonight where you can find some other cute guys."

You're getting close to the front of the line, so you have to decide pretty quickly.

"Yolo," Tasha says. "I mean, seriously, yolo."

You do only live once. Which means, time for a surf lesson.

"Good luck with Lobsterman," you tell Tasha. And you follow the arrow on the sign toward the surf lessons.

When you get there, an impossibly tall guy with impossibly sharp cheekbones and long wavy sun-bleached hair is zipping up a bag of stuff. He's wearing a wetsuit unzipped and hanging down around his waist. His chest is bare and hairless. His face is close to hairless, too—just a few patches of prickles—which makes you realize that he's probably closer to your age than you initially thought.

"May I help you?" he asks in French-accented English.

This must be Jean Paul.

"I think so?" you say, cursing yourself for turning the declaration into a question. "I saw the sign for surf lessons. Are you closed for the day?"

Jean Paul sweeps his eyes over you from your ponytail down to your toe polish. "I was going to close," he tells you, "but perhaps I can stay open for one more lesson. One half hour is forty dollars."

You'd brought your wallet with you to the lobster-roll truck, and you know you have forty dollars in cash in there.

"Okay," you say. "A half hour sounds good. I've never done this before."

"A virgin!" Jean Paul says, and laughs. "I'll call you Mary."

You feel your cheeks turn pink. You know that he was just talking about this being your first time surfing, but that word made your mind go somewhere else, and you're pretty sure it made his go to that same place. And once the image of Jean Paul naked is in your head, it's hard to get it out.

"Mary's fine with me," you say, "but what should I call you?"

He shrugs. "You can call me Jean Paul," he says. "That's my name."

"Nope," you tell him. "Not fair. If you give me a fake name, I get to give you one." You try to think of something clever, something slightly risqué, but nothing is coming to you. "How about Poseidon?" you finally say.

"You have made me a god!" Jean Paul responds. "*Poséidon, le dieu de la mer à la mythologie grecque.* I studied him at the university last year. It was a required class for all who were—I forget the word in English—freshman?"

You feel yourself blush even more as you nod. You were just trying to think of something having to do with the ocean. Also, it sounds extra sexy when he speaks French. Nothing like the way your French teacher sounds at school.

"If I'm Poseidon, then I'm changing your name," he says. "You're Amphitrite."

"Poseidon's wife?" you say.

"*Absolument*," he answers. "Now, Amphitrite, I will teach you to surf!"

Jean Paul gives you a wetsuit to zip over your bikini—the kind with short sleeves that comes to your knees—and locks your stuff up in a little set of lockers under the surf school tent. He zips his wetsuit up, too, which is really too bad because now his chest is covered. Then he pulls a longboard off the rack and hands it to you.

"Okay," he says, "put the board under your arm and follow me."

It's a little awkward and ungainly, but you do what he says and follow him closer to the water. He puts his board down on the sand, and you put yours down next to him.

"First," he says, "we practice getting up on the board. You are right-handed, yes?"

You nod.

"*Bon*," he says. He lies down on the board and tells you to watch him. "It's a four count. *Un*, you push up with your arms. *Deux*, you move your right leg forward. *Trois*, you bring your left leg in front of your right. *Quatre*, you stand up! Then use your arms to balance. Let's do it together."

You mimic everything Jean Paul does, and count along with him, hoping your French accent isn't too terrible. You know your *quatre* doesn't sound like his, for sure.

"Good, now faster!" he says.

You go faster, even though your shoulder muscles are starting to hurt from *un*—the push-up maneuver. Once Jean Paul is happy with your stand-up speed, he wraps the surfboard's Velcro ankle strap around your leg. You shiver when his fingers brush your skin.

"Now, the ocean!" he says. "I'll hold your board, and when a small wave is coming, I'll tell you when to stand and let you go."

You take a deep breath. You totally got the hang of standing on land, but standing in the water seems like another thing entirely.

"It's okay if you fall," Jean Paul says. He must've seen the fear on your face. "Besides, I named you a sea goddess. You were born for this, Amphitrite."

You screw your courage to the sticking place, the way your tennis coach/ninth-grade English teacher always told you to do before a match. "All right, Poseidon," you say. "I'm ready."

"*Fantastique!*" Jean Paul says.

He leaves his surfboard in the sand and heads into the ocean. You follow behind him, your board Velcroed to your leg.

"This is good," he tells you when the water is about waist deep. "Now, you lie down on your board, and get ready, and I'll tell you when to go."

He hangs on to the back of your surfboard and you balance on it like it's a raft, but you're not relaxed at all. Your arms are tense, your palms ready to push up at a moment's notice.

"Okay," Jean Paul says. "It's coming . . . and . . . go!"

You count in your head, *un, deux, trois, quatre,* and you're up! You're totally standing on a surfboard! You're surfing! And then just as quickly as you're up, you feel the board wobble and you're not balancing quite right, and you go tumbling into the water. But as you pop up, you know there's a huge grin on your face, because that felt awesome. It felt more than awesome. For a few seconds there, you really were Amphitrite, goddess of the sea.

"You okay?" Jean Paul shouts. "That was great for your first time! You made it up! That's more than a lot of people can do."

You walk through the water back to where you started. "I'm great!" you say. *"Fantastique!"*

"You are," he says, laughing. "You want to do it again?"

"Definitely," you tell him.

You climb on board and wait again, and then Jean Paul lets go and the wave comes and you're up again, and down again. You do it over and over and over, more times than you can count, but you can't seem to stay up for more than a few seconds.

"What am I doing wrong?" you ask Jean Paul.

"It's here," he says, touching your stomach. "Your core."

You feel butterflies right where he's touched you.

"And keep your legs loose. Not too tight. You need to feel the board and compensate."

You take a breath. "Okay, one more time," you say.

You're pretty sure you've gone way over your half-hour lesson, but Jean Paul hasn't said anything, so you don't, either.

You climb on the board and get ready. He lets you go, you count to four—in French—and you're up! You concentrate on keeping your legs loose and your core tight. The board moves, and you compensate. You do! It moves again, and you're still standing. Your arms are out at your sides for extra balance, and you ride the wave all the way to shore. When you hit the sand, you jump off the board.

You turn around to look for Jean Paul, and you see him running toward you.

"*C'est magnifique!*" he says, as he lifts you up in his arms. "Amphitrite, that was perfect!"

You wrap your arms around his shoulders, and he kisses you on the cheek before he puts you back down again.

"That felt fabulous!" you tell him.

He looks at you out of the corner of his eye.

"Riding the wave, or being in my arms?" he asks.

You laugh. "Both," you admit.

"I thought perhaps you would say that," he says. "But I want my arms to feel better than surfing, so let's try again."

Your heart hammers in your chest as he lifts you up once more, but this time he presses his mouth to yours and catches your bottom lip between his teeth. He teases you with his tongue, and then slides it into your mouth. You wonder if in addition to being a sea god, he's also a kissing god.

Tasha was right, you only live once, and you're so glad that during this one time you live you get to be wrapped in the arms of a sexy French surfer and kiss him on the weekend after your sixteenth birthday.

CONGRATULATIONS!
YOU'VE FOUND YOUR HAPPY ENDING!

"SURE," you say. "I'll keep you and Gonzo company. But I hope we don't run into too many cars."

Nik smiles. "Me, too," he says. His grin is wider than it was before, and you notice that his teeth are remarkably white and straight. You wonder for a second if he wore braces and decide that he probably did. Then you decide that you like that. Braces humble a person. Make it so a person never gets too cocky.

"Let me just quickly text Tasha, in case she wakes up while I'm gone," you say. You pull out your phone and write:

> Found boy to flirt with. Neighbor. Nik.
>
> Be back sometime.

Then you unlatch the lock on the gate and let

yourself out. Gonzo jumps up on your legs and grabs the hem of your bathing suit cover-up in his teeth.

"Gonzo! Stop it!" Nik says, tapping the dog on the nose.

Gonzo lets go of your cover-up.

"He's feisty!" you say, and Nik blushes again.

"I'm sorry. Really, I don't know what's gotten into him." Nik wraps Gonzo's leash around his hand a few times so that the dog can't move more than a few inches away from him.

"So how long have you had Gonzo?" you ask, figuring that's as good a place to start as any.

"Actually not that long," Nik tells you. "He's an old guy—seven or eight, they think—but he was a rescue. A car must've done something bad to him, or maybe his previous owner did, I don't know. Sometimes I wish there was a doggie therapist he could talk to who could help him out."

You laugh. "I love that idea! When I was a kid, I had a crazy hamster. He could've used a hamster therapist, I bet."

"I've met quite a few crazy hamsters," Nik tells you as you walk down the street. "Maybe it's the wheel. You know, going round and round and round and getting nowhere might make me a little crazy, too."

"Poor guys," you say, holding in your laughter. "And don't forget about the goldfish, swimming in circles all day!"

Nik has a very serious look on his face. "I know! They must get so dizzy. And exhausted!"

You look back at him equally seriously. And then the two of you burst out laughing.

"Are you into animals?" you finally ask after the laughter subsides.

He stops to scratch Gonzo behind the ears before he says, "Yes." And adds, "Actually, I'm going to major in animal science in college next year. I want to be a veterinarian."

"No way," you say, mostly because that's one of the coolest future job plans you've heard.

"Way," he says, with a laugh. "What about you? Do you know what you want to major in?"

You shake your head. "I'm only in high school. I'll be a junior next year," you tell him. "I'm not sure yet."

He nods. "It's a serious decision. I mean, not like life or death serious. Actually, that was the wrong word. It's important, not serious."

Now it's your turn to nod. You decide that you like the fact that Nik searched around until he found the exact right word to explain how he felt about the college-major decision. And you like how much he likes animals. And how funny he is. And how he's incredibly handsome. Sexy even. In fact, he's one of the all-around coolest guys you've ever met.

"Did you always want to be a vet?" you ask him.

A car goes by, and Gonzo barks like it's going out of style. Nik rubs him on the head, but it doesn't seem to make a difference.

"I always wanted to work with animals," Nik said. "And my dad's a human doctor, so being an animal doctor seemed to make sense. Though I think my dad's a little disappointed I don't want to follow his path."

"Parents get disappointed in the weirdest things," you say. It's kind of amazing how much Nik is sharing with you, but it doesn't feel strange. It feels as if he should be telling you all of this, as if you've known each other for ages, not just a few minutes. So you respond in kind.

"I can tell my dad's really bummed that I don't like golf," you say. "Or math. The two things he spends the most time doing are two things that make me so bored I'd rather watch grass grow than talk about them. He pretends he's not disappointed, but I can tell he wishes it were different. That I was different."

Nik nods. "I know how you feel. I think parents want to see themselves in their kids so badly that they forget they've created a different, new person."

"Sometimes I wish I had a brother or sister who loved math and golf, and then I wouldn't feel so bad that I don't." You've never admitted this to anyone, not even to Tasha, but it feels good to say it to Nik. There's something about him that makes you want to tell him all your secrets. He seems like he'd understand. And would never make fun of you, even if your secrets were silly.

"That would be nice," he says, and you can tell he's thinking about having a brother or sister who wanted to be a people doctor so he wouldn't have to feel bad.

You've reached the end of the street, where it runs into a marina. "I guess we should turn around," Nik says to you.

"Yeah, I guess," you answer, but you'd rather he invite you to have an ice cream cone with him at the marina. You think about extending the invite yourself, but decide not to, mostly because you'd be too embarrassed if he said no. Even if he turned you down in the nicest way possible.

You start walking back up the street, and another car goes by. This time you crouch and pet Gonzo, trying to calm him down, and it seems like maybe it's working.

"Are you a secret dog whisperer?" Nik asks, squinting at you.

"You got me," you say.

Gonzo pulls against his leash, trying to jump into your arms. You pet him again and then stand. "Want me to hold that for a while?" you ask, indicating the leash.

Nik shrugs. "Sure." He slips the leash off his hand and onto yours. When his fingers touch your fingers, you feel a tingle go through you, like getting splashed with ice-cold water on a crazy hot day.

You look at Nik and notice the soft pinkness of his lips against his white teeth and olive-dark skin. You wish for a moment that you were a good artist, because if you were, you'd draw him right then.

As soon as Nik lets go of the leash, you wrap your fingers around it tight, letting Gonzo run a few feet ahead of you two.

"Nik," you say. And then stop. You're not sure what you want to say exactly, but there's something about him, something kind and caring and vulnerable that makes you want to get to know him better. It makes you want to call your parents and ask if you can stay at the beach the whole summer, just so you can spend time with Nik.

"Yeah?" he asks, looking at you with a question in his eyes.

Before you can open your mouth again, a car comes racing down the street and Gonzo goes bonkers. He yaps and yaps and runs toward the car and away from the car, making circles around you and Nik. Nik bends to stop him, but Gonzo's too fast, and you can already see the leash getting tangled in knots around your feet and Nik's. Nik goes to take a step, but before you can warn him about the tangled leash, he trips and falls right into you. You try your hardest to keep your balance, but you wobble, and then the two of you tumble to the ground, a pile of arms, legs, leash, and dog.

The way you've fallen, you're somehow on the bottom of the pile and Nik is on top, his stomach resting on yours. His chin is inches from your lips. His eyes look down at you.

"Hey," you say to him.

"Hey," he says back.

But neither of you moves. It's like there's this

force field keeping you in place.

You get the feeling that Nik's not the kind of person to make the first move, so if you want to kiss him, you're going to have to do it yourself. You take a deep breath, tilt your chin up so your lips are aligned, and then move your head slightly forward.

Your lips meet his softly, and the tingle you felt from his fingers touching you before spreads throughout your entire body. Nik pulls himself up into a sitting position and tugs you up with him, so now you're on the sidewalk, kissing, his arms wrapped around you.

The kiss gets deeper, and he runs his teeth along your bottom lip. In spite of the summer heat, you shiver.

"Nik," you whisper.

He kisses you harder.

A car goes by, and Gonzo barks, but you can barely hear it. All your senses are wrapped up in Nik—the taste, the feel, the smell, the sound of him. It's like the rest of the world has disappeared.

He catches his fingers in your hair and breaks off the kiss.

"Wow," he says.

"Yeah, wow," you agree.

And you know, deep down inside, the way you know to stay away from the edge of a cliff, the way you jump at loud noises, that this isn't the only time you're going to see Nik. You feel as if you've connected with him. Like he understands you. And like you understand him. You can tell that he'd be more than a good boyfriend—he'd be a good friend, too. And that if you have it your way, he's going to be a part of your life for a long time to come.

He leans in to kiss you again, and you think, *Thank goodness I didn't kiss Tyler Grant. Tyler Grant couldn't hold a candle to this boy.*

You stand up and hold Nik's hand. Gonzo dances around you both, looking for someone to pay attention to him, but you and Nik only have eyes for each other.

"I'm glad you came to the beach this weekend," he whispers.

"Me, too," you tell him, squeezing his hand. "Me, too."

CONGRATULATIONS!
YOU'VE FOUND YOUR HAPPY ENDING!

YOU sit back down in your chaise lounge by the pool as quietly as you can so you don't wake Tasha, but all the trying to be quiet ends up being a waste, because when you lean back, the hook keeping the backrest in place comes undone, and it clanks onto the brick patio. Tasha wakes up.

"Are you okay?" she asks, snapping up in her chair.

"I'm fine," you tell her, as you get up to see what happened. "Minor chair malfunction, that's all. You can go back to sleep if you want."

She stretches, and you can already see a tan line forming at the edge of her bikini bottoms. Tasha sees it, too.

"Would you mind reapplying me?" she asks, holding out a bottle of sunscreen.

"Not at all," you say.

Tasha squirts some sunscreen in your hand and some in her own. She starts on the front of her body, and you move to her back. "What SPF is this?" you ask her.

"Thirty," she replies. "I always start with thirty at the beginning of the summer and then work down to fifteen once I have a base tan."

You wonder if that's a real thing: a base tan.

As you rub the lotion under her bikini strap, she keeps talking. "You know, I read an article that said that all the higher SPFs—the ones like fifty and eighty and whatever—it's just marketing. They don't work any better than thirty."

"Is that true?" you ask her. You're a bit incredulous. How would the companies be allowed to say that the sun protection factor was higher if it's really just a lie?

Tasha shrugs. "That's what the article said. I didn't fact-check it or anything. Want me to do you?"

You nod, and Tasha reapplies sunscreen to your back while you do your front. The fastest way to ruin a beach vacation is to get sunburned the first afternoon you're there. You know this from experience.

When you're done with the sunscreen, Tasha

picks up a copy of *Entertainment Weekly* you've brought out. You grab a copy of *People*.

"Okay," Tasha says. "Here's the game: whichever one of us finds the least flattering picture of a celebrity in our magazine wins. Go!"

That seems sort of mean. "How about most flattering," you say.

Tasha rolls her eyes at you. "You're really nice, you know that?" she asks.

Sometimes you are, but not always. You don't say that, though. What you say is, "I just wanted two chances to win."

"Fine," Tasha says. "Most flattering and least flattering. And winner decides where we eat tonight."

"Deal," you say, opening your magazine.

But before you can get too far in, you hear the gate to the street open. You turn around, and two muscular guys without shirts walk into the backyard.

"Um," you whisper, "Tasha? Who are they? Did you order them for my birthday?"

She looks up from her magazine, and her face lights up. "Luke! Scott! Hey!" she says. Then whispers to you, "They're the pool guys. Brothers. Their dad owns the pool-cleaning company. We've used their family's company for years."

"Hey, Tasha!" one of the brothers says as he puts down the pool-cleaning equipment. "Our dad said you guys wouldn't be here until next week."

"That's when my parents are coming, and when I'm coming officially," she tells him. "I'm here unofficially with my cousin. It was just her sixteenth birthday."

"Hi, there, Tasha's cousin," the first brother says, walking toward you. "And happy birthday. I'm Scott."

You shake his hand. "Hi, and thanks," you say.

"And I'm Luke." The second brother walks over to the rest of you. "I turned sixteen a few months back, so I guess we're in the same grade. You thinking about college yet?"

You groan. "I should be," you say, pulling a towel over your head.

Luke laughs and sits down on the edge of your chaise lounge. "Tell me about it. Scott's heading off to UMass in the fall, and now my parents are all on my case."

"I want her to come to school with me," Tasha tells the brothers. "It would be so much fun!"

"Maybe," you tell Tasha. "I haven't ruled it out."

"But you haven't ruled it in, either," she says. "It's all rather tragic."

Scott laughs, and Luke smiles. You smile, too.

"Hey," Luke says, picking up your *People* magazine. "Have you done the crossword puzzle yet?"

You squint at him. "How do you even know that *People* magazine has a crossword puzzle?"

He shrugs. "It's totally not just for chicks. They have great movie recommendations and stuff."

He flips to the crossword puzzle page. "I know the first one," he says. "You got a pen?"

You hand him a pen from Tasha's bag and then can't help but look over his shoulder at the puzzle. After he fills in number one across, you give him number one down. And number two down. Then he gets number five across. And you get five down.

"I don't mean to brag," Luke says, "but I think you and I are pretty much pwning this crossword puzzle."

You nod, with a mock-serious expression on your face. "We take no prisoners. We capture and kill all crossword puzzles we find."

Everything's quiet for a second, and you realize that Scott and Tasha are looking at you and Luke. Scott clears his throat.

"Luke, as much as you're enjoying your take-no-prisoners crossword-puzzle session, we actually have work to do here."

Luke jumps off your chaise lounge. "Right!" he says. "Okay, let's go."

You look at Tasha, and she does an eyebrow raise. Then she mouths the word: *Later?* You bite your lip to let her know you got her message. But now you have to decide if you want to act on it.

Turn to page 125 if you invite the brothers over for dinner later.

- - - - -

Turn to page 139 if you forget about the boys and ask Tasha to help you finish the crossword puzzle.

"AND thanks for the bench tip, too," you add, about to follow after Tasha, who has started to head in that general direction.

"Wait!" he says. You turn back, and he leans out of the truck and hands you a double-chocolate-chip cookie. "I thought you might like this, too. My mom makes these. She makes all of the cookies we sell, but I think this one is her best."

"Wow," you say. "I can't wait to give it a try. You know . . . I'll be around for most of the afternoon, so if you get off work and want to say hi . . ."

His megawatt smile lights up his face again. "I'll find you," he says. "I'll definitely come and find you. I'm Jackson, by the way."

You feel your own face break into a grin. "Okay then," you say. "I'll see you later, Jackson."

You find Tasha on the bench that Jackson suggested and sit down next to her. She's already eating, and as she does, her eyes are fixed on a muscular fisherman in a pair of cut-off jean shorts.

"Tasty?" you ask.

"The roll or the guy unloading fish?" she answers.

You laugh. "Both?"

"Both quite tasty. And nice work getting us free chips."

You take a bite of your lobster roll. It's salty and lobstery, and the bread is toasted to perfection. Delicious. After you swallow you say, "I didn't do much—I think he was just in a good mood."

Tasha takes another bite and swallows. "Jealous," she says. "But how hot is that fisherman?"

"Very," you answer, even though he's not really doing it for you. It may sound silly, but you've never been into the way guys look in cut-off jean shorts.

Tasha's fisherman finishes unloading his catch and heads off the boat while you finish your lobster roll and some of the potato chips. Her face falls.

"Want to head home soon?" she asks, as you take a bite of Jackson's mom's cookie. It's fantastic. Because of the weather, the chips are a little gooey, which makes them extra wonderful.

"Mmm," you say, "Tash, you have to taste this."

She takes a bite. "Oh my God. I could eat, like, a hundred of these. I'm glad we only have one. This is sinful."

Just as you're licking final bits of chocolate from your fingers, Jackson comes over.

"Hey!" he says. "I'm so glad I found you two here! One of the guys just came over from my dad's restaurant with refills on chips and cookies. I told him to man the lobster-roll truck while I came to find you. Any chance you want to help me unload?"

You look over at Tasha. "We can head home after you're done," she says. "No rush. I can relax back at our towels."

You look up at Jackson's blueberry eyes and huge grin.

Turn to page 143 if you decide to help him unload his truck.

- - - - -

Turn to page 15 if you decide to head back to Tasha's parents' house.

YOU think for a second about inviting Lobster Roll Guy to hang out later, but decide that he had a lot of opportunities to ask you, and if he didn't, it was probably for a reason. Maybe he has a girlfriend—the Crab Queen or something. The Prawn Princess. Though if he does have a girlfriend, someone should probably let her know that he flirts with the people on the line for his lobster rolls.

You trail after Tasha and sit down next to her. She takes a bite of her lobster roll, and as she does, her eyes focus on a muscular fisherman in a pair of cut-off jean shorts.

"Tasty?" you ask.

"The roll or the guy unloading fish?" she answers.

You laugh. "Both?"

"Both quite tasty. And nice work getting us free chips."

You take a bite of your lobster roll. It's salty and lobstery, and the bread is toasted to perfection. Delicious. After you swallow you say, "I didn't do much—I think he was just in a good mood. Or maybe he liked flirting with me."

Tasha takes another bite and swallows. "Jealous," she says. "But how hot is that fisherman?"

"Very," you answer, even though he's not really doing it for you. It may sound silly, but you've never been into the way guys look in cut-off jean shorts.

Tasha's fisherman looks up at you both. Tasha waves. He waves back. Then another fisherman comes up next to the first one. This guy isn't wearing jean shorts. He's wearing cargo shorts and a white T-shirt, and his hair is in a ponytail. As far as you're concerned, he's much cuter than the fisherman Tasha's been staring at. This guy waves at you.

---

*Turn to page 151 if you wave back
and chat with the fisherman.*

- - - - -

*Turn to page 87 if you've had enough
of the beach and want to head home.*

YOU look over at Luke. He and his brother have a
pool vacuum out and are lowering it into the deep
end of the pool. His arm muscles pop as he does it.
Tyler Grant doesn't have arm muscles like that. You
turn to Tasha.

"Let's do it," you say.

A smile spreads across her face. "This is gonna be
awesome," she says.

You watch as Tasha gets up and walks over to
Scott and Luke. Scott's working the vacuum and
Luke has a pH kit in his hand, about to check the
chemical balance of the water.

"Hey, guys," she says.

Both brothers stop what they're doing and look
at her. "Hey," Scott says. "Do you need something?"

Tasha shakes her head. "No, not at all. But my

cousin and I, we have the house to ourselves tonight, and we thought it would be fun to have a small barbecue. Supersmall. Like, the two of us and the two of you. Any chance you're free?"

Luke and Scott exchange a look. You can't quite tell what it means. But then Scott turns back to Tasha and says, "Yeah, we're free. Our last pool job should end around six. We can shower and then be over here around seven?"

Tasha nods. "Sounds good. And we'll take care of all the food. So just bring yourselves."

"Got it," Luke says, as he goes back to testing the pool water.

Even though he's playing it cool, you can see him smiling. Scott's smiling, too.

Tasha drags you back into the house and closes the sliding glass door behind you, separating you both from the brothers.

"This is going to be awesome!" she says. "I've never thrown a barbecue dinner party before!"

You laugh. "Tash, I don't know if this is quite a dinner party. It's us and two guys. I mean, I don't think there's a ton to prepare."

"Of course there is!" Tasha says. "Let's make a list."

Tasha pulls out her cell phone and opens a blank note screen.

"Okay, first we need a list of food," she says. "We said barbecue, so we need hamburgers and hot dogs."

"Both?" you ask.

"Both," she says firmly. "What else do my parents make when they do a barbecue?"

You think back to your summer trips to Tasha's beach house. "Corn," you say. "And mushrooms. And tiny potatoes wrapped in foil."

"Ooh! Yeah! The tiny potatoes. Let's make those. I don't think we need the corn or the mushrooms."

In thinking back to those summer barbecues, you realize that Tasha was never the one grilling. She was never even close to her father while he was grilling. "I hate to ask this," you say, "but do you know how to make all that stuff?"

Tasha shrugs. "How hard could it be? Let's get the ingredients. We'll figure it out from there."

✳

AN hour later, you and Tasha make it back from the grocery store with a bag filled with hot dogs, hamburgers, buns, potatoes, tinfoil, olive oil, sauerkraut, pickles, tomatoes, onions, orange soda, Diet Coke, and medium-size watermelon for dessert.

"So, what do we do now?" you ask Tasha. You've never made a barbecue by yourself before, either.

"I think," Tasha says, "that we put all of this away, shower, and get dressed. You know, so we look cute while we flip burgers."

"I have a bad feeling about this," you tell her.

She just laughs. "Whatever, it'll be fun," she says, heading up to her bathroom.

You follow her orders and shower, too. You look at the three dresses you brought and decide that the light green-and-white patterned shift dress looks very barbecue-appropriate. You add a pair of gold hoop earrings and twist your hair up into a bun on top of your head. You slide into gold leather sandals and add a bangle on your wrist.

Tasha pokes her head into your room. "Ooh, nice choice!" she says. She has on silk patterned shorts and a white strapless top with platform sandals. The cork-soled kind. Her hair is teased in the front and swept into a high ponytail, and she has red beaded earrings dangling from her ears.

"You, too," you tell her. You pull out your makeup case and twist open your black mascara.

"I came to borrow your blush," Tasha tells you. "I forgot mine."

"Have at it," you say while brushing the wand over your eyelashes.

Tasha riffles through your makeup case and pulls out your blush. "Aren't you excited?" she asks as she brushes it across her cheekbones and the line of her nose.

"I guess," you say. "But I'm a little worried about the actual barbecuing part."

"Piece of cake!" she says, grabbing for your bright red lipstick. You don't mind because you weren't going to wear it anyway. You reach for your hot pink shimmer gloss.

"We'll see," you say, opening your mouth to slick the gloss on.

After you and Tasha are all dressed, you head to the kitchen.

"Baby potatoes," Tasha says, pulling the bag out of the fridge. "I've seen my dad make these. You just get a little square of tinfoil, drizzle on some olive oil, add salt and pepper, and wrap it up. Easy."

You pick up a baby potato. "I think we have to wash them first," you say, looking at the dirt on the potato skin.

"Oooh, good call." Tasha hands you the bag of potatoes. "That can be your job."

You start washing baby potatoes, and before you know it there are splotches of dirty water on your dress.

"Tash," you say, "I think maybe we should've made the food and then gotten dressed."

She looks over at your dress, giving it a very serious assessment. "No one can tell. You're fine."

You make the executive decision to wash only ten baby potatoes. You figure you and Tasha won't eat more than two each, and then each guy might eat three. So ten is enough.

"But we have a whole bag!" Tasha says.

"They'll keep," you tell her. But the truth is, you have no idea. How long can potatoes stay in a pantry before they go bad?

She says fine, and then starts putting potatoes in foil and drizzling them in olive oil.

"Oh eff!" she says, looking down at her top. "I drizzled olive oil on my shirt."

"What did I tell you?" you say.

She gives you the evilest look in her repertoire. "Well, let's see how the rest of the cooking goes. We can always change before they get here."

The hamburgers and hot dogs don't require much attention, and the rest of the stuff is pretty much just condiments.

"I think it's time to grill," you say.

Tasha nods. "Okay, so my dad, um, he puts little brick things into the grill, and then he lights it with a really long match, and in a few minutes it's ready to cook on."

You and Tasha go to the pool house and find the charcoal bricks. They're in a huge bag, and it takes both of you to carry it. Now there are black charcoal smudges on your dress to go along with the dirty potato water. You dump some little bricks into the bottom of the grill, get the really long grill matches, and try to get it to catch. It's not working. Tasha tries three matches. You try two more.

"We're obviously doing something wrong," you tell her.

"Ya think?" she answers, rolling her eyes.

"I think this calls for some smartphone searching," you say, ignoring her eye roll.

You search for "how do I make a grill start with charcoal bricks?" And the first few answers tell you that you need lighter fluid. Or a thing called a charcoal chimney. You pass this information on to

Tasha. She curses, heads back to the pool house, and storms back with a bottle of lighter fluid. Her hair is now falling out of its ponytail and curling up around her face. She would *not* be happy if she knew, but you don't tell her. She's stressed enough as it is without having to worry about her hair.

"How much does it say I should use?" she asks.

You consult your phone. "It doesn't say," you tell her. "It just says that it should be evenly spread on all the coals, and that you should let it soak in for thirty seconds before trying to light it again."

Tasha wipes her forehead with her hand, smudging it with black charcoal. "Well, here goes nothing," she says, and drips lighter fluid onto the coals. You count Mississippis out loud, and when you get to thirty, she lights a match and touches it to the charcoal. It goes up in flames, and then you see the coals starting to burn white.

"We have liftoff!" you say.

"You are such a dork," Tasha answers. "Does your phone say how long to wait until we start cooking?"

You check. "Fifteen minutes, or when all the coals start looking ashy and white."

"Okay," she says. "I'm going to change. You, too?"

You look down at your dress. "Me, too," you sigh.

"Oh, and make sure you get the smudge on your forehead."

"Eff!" she says. "Thanks."

Fifteen minutes later you come back and open the grill. The coals seem to have died down. It's not very hot.

"We messed up again," you say.

Even with her new outfit, new ponytail, and new makeup, Tasha still looks harried. She grits her teeth.

"What time is it?" she asks you.

You look at your phone. "They'll be here in ten minutes."

"Eff!" she says again, louder this time.

The doorbell rings. It has to be the boys. You smooth down the blue A-line dress you're now wearing. Not quite as nice as your last one, but not so bad, either.

"I can't believe they're here! Who arrives somewhere early?" she asks, staring forlornly at the grill.

"People who can't wait for their plans," you say. "Maybe they can help. I'll get the door. You set the table."

Tasha nods. Whenever the two of you are together, she's usually in charge, but the nonworking grill seemed to be too much for her to handle, so you took the lead. You walk through to the door and open it. Scott and Luke are there in T-shirts, shorts, button-downs, and leather flip-flops. They both look deliciously handsome, with their cheeks pinked from their day in the sun.

"Come in!" you say. "We're having a little bit of grill trouble, but we're so happy you're here!"

"Grill trouble?" Luke asks. You nod and ask if he might be able to help. "I'll take a look," he says.

You send Scott over to help Tasha set the table and lead Luke out to the grill. You explain all of the things you did and what happened. He examines the grill's cover and the charcoal inside.

"Ah," he says. "You didn't vent the top. And I'm guessing you didn't use quite enough lighter fluid. You've really gotta douse those things."

He flicks something on the cover, pours a ton of lighter fluid on the charcoal, and then hands you the long matches. "Would you like to do the honors?" he asks.

You smile, flick the match, and touch it onto the charcoal. The whole thing goes up in a whoosh of flame and then starts burning all over.

"You did it!" you say, turning to Luke.

"We both did it," he says, smiling at you.

You smile back. "Well, I don't think I can take much credit, but thank you."

You grab the spatula and the plate of burgers. You're not completely sure what to do next, or where to put the burgers on the grill. Luke must sense your hesitation because he comes up behind you and says, "Let's do this together, too."

He wraps his hand around the one you have on the spatula and slides the flat part under a burger. The two of you move the burger to the grill and then he tips it into the middle of the cooking section. You do all the burgers like this, together, and then move on to the hot dogs.

"I'm glad you're here to help," you say. You can feel the heat of Luke's body against your back, and his hand is still wrapped around yours on the spatula.

"I'm glad you invited me to help," he says, and his breath tickles the back of your neck. It gives you the chills.

"What do you think Tasha and Scott are doing?" you ask, not because you really care all that much, but because it gives you something to say. Something to distract you from the goose bumps that Luke's closeness is causing.

He looks around. "They seem to have disappeared," he tells you. "Maybe they went inside?"

You laugh. Tasha really has a one-track mind. "Yeah," you say. "They probably did."

"Which means we're all alone out here." Every time his mouth forms a W, his breath puffs against your neck. The second time, it makes you shiver.

"Are you cold?" he asks, still behind you.

"Maybe," you answer. Though really, you're not cold at all. You're standing in front of a hot grill.

He slides his arms around you and brings his body in closer so its pressed against yours. "Better?" he asks.

You shiver again. "Much better," you tell him, as you lean farther back into his arms.

Then you feel his lips on the side of your neck. He's kissing your neck. And it feels warm and sexy and incredible.

"Even better," you say, but your voice is quiet now.

You turn in Luke's arms so you're face-to-face now. The kiss that felt so wonderful on your neck feels wonderful times a million on your lips. Luke's strong arms pull you close, and you feel as if you're melting against him.

In that moment, you forget about Tasha, you

forget about the barbecue, you forget about the hamburgers and hot dogs and the grill in front of you. The food could burn, and it wouldn't matter. Because Luke's kiss is all you'd need to keep you feeling satisfied the whole night long.

CONGRATULATIONS!
YOU'VE FOUND YOUR HAPPY ENDING!

YOU look over at Luke. He and his brother have a pool vacuum out and are lowering it into the deep end of the pool. His arm muscles pop as he does it. His brown hair is falling in his eyes. He has dimples. He's pretty much fourteen flavors of adorable. But you're not really feeling it.

"I was looking forward to a quiet night tonight," you tell Tasha. "Maybe we can host a barbecue tomorrow night? We'll see how we feel?"

"Sure," she says. "No problem." Though you do notice her eyes darting to Scott and lingering there.

You look down at your crossword puzzle. You're stuck on "A 2013 film that completes Richard Linklater's romantic drama trilogy about Jesse and Céline."

"Tash," you say, "you know about movies. Do

you know the answer to seven down?" You pass the crossword puzzle her way.

"*Before Midnight*," she tells you. And then adds, "Have you seen those?"

You shake your head.

She sits up on her lounge chair. "Oh, you have to! They're so good! Want to see if we can stream them tonight and have a marathon? Maybe invite Jade? She loves those movies."

You nod. "Yeah, that sounds good." A night home with Tasha and Jade is really more what you had in mind. You can always go out and party tomorrow night, if you want.

You keep flipping through your *People*, reading articles and doing that game where you circle things that aren't in one picture but are in the other. It's always harder than you expect it to be to find the differences between the two.

After that you close *People* and pick up *Teen Vogue*. There's a big headline on the cover that says "Are You Ready to Find Your True Love?"

You flip to the contents page and then turn to the article. There's a quiz, and you decide to take it.

The first question asks what you're looking for when you go out on a date. The choices are: (a) some fun, (b) someone you connect with on many levels, or (c) the person you hope to spend the rest of your life with. You think about your train conversation with Tasha and choose (b)—but then you're not so sure. Maybe it's (a). Or maybe it's both. You circle both and decide that you'll average the two answers and count that as your points. Then the quiz asks how much you think about sharing a future with any guy you go out on a date with: (a) not at all, (b) sometimes, or (c) I can't stop thinking about it! You decide to average (a) and (b) for this one, too. Though you're leaning a little more toward (a). Then it asks about how much you have to connect with someone before getting physical: (a) as long as he's hot, that's fine with me, (b) I have to think he's got a great personality, too, or (c) I would never kiss anyone unless I respected him enough to marry him. For this one you circle (a)—that's what the kissing challenge was about after all. Then it asks how well you know yourself: (a) I'm figuring out who I am, (b) I'm on my way, but still need to work a few things out, or (c) I know myself inside and out—I know where I'm going and how I can get there. For this one you circle (a) for sure. It's (a) times a million.

After tallying up your score—(a)s get 1 point,

(b)s get 2 points, and (c)s get 3—you find the paragraph that's supposed to pertain to you and read through what it means. The gist of it is: you're not ready for a serious relationship right now; you need to figure yourself out first, and once you do that, you'll be better at connecting with someone else romantically.

You think about that. Maybe *Teen Vogue* is right. Maybe before you start flirting with boys and kissing boys and trying to date boys, you should know who you are and what you want and where you stand. That sounds like good advice, actually. You want to know what you're capable of and feel sure of who you are.

"I choose me," you say out loud.

"Hmm?" Tasha asks. Her eyes are closed, and she's soaking up the sun.

"Nothing," you say, smiling to yourself. Because on the inside, it doesn't feel like nothing at all. It feels like everything. Before you find a boy, you vow to find yourself.

CONGRATULATIONS!
YOU'VE FOUND YOUR HAPPY ENDING!

"YOU sure you don't mind?" you ask Tasha.

"Not at all," she says, getting up from the bench. "I'll be at the towel when you're ready to go."

"So that's a yes?" Jackson asks.

"That's a yes," you say.

You walk with him off the wharf and back to the parking lot.

"So how did you like the lobster roll?" he asks you.

"Oh, it was great," you say. "And so was your mom's cookie. Does she run a bakery or something?"

He shakes his head. "My dad runs the Lobster Shack down the road," he says. "And my mom's been cooking there with him since they got married. She always wanted to bake, though, so about five years into it started making the cookies they sell there, too."

You've reached the truck with all the stuff in it—you know because it's big and red and has the words **LOBSTER SHACK** painted on the side with an address and a phone number.

"It must be cool to have a lobster restaurant in the family. Do you eat lobster, like, every day?" you ask Jackson.

He laughs and jumps into the back of the truck. "I'll hand the cookies and chips out to you," he says. "Can you pile the boxes on the dolly over there?" He's pointing to a metal thing with wheels right next to the truck.

You nod. "Sure," you say. "As long as they're not too heavy."

"The chips are really light," Jackson tells you as he hands you a box. You realize he's totally right, and put the box on the dolly.

"And I don't eat lobster every day," he says. "My parents and I limit ourselves so we won't get sick of it. Good plan, I think. So it's still a treat, even for us. Besides, there are some times of year that are better for catching lobsters than others, so it's not like we have hundreds of lobsters every day all year round."

You'd never thought about that, but it makes sense. "So when did your dad come up with this truck idea?" you ask. "I don't remember it from last summer, but I was only here for a weekend, so I might not have noticed."

Jackson does his megasmile thing again, and his blueberry eyes twinkle a little. "This is the first summer!" he says. "It was my idea, so my dad said I could run it. I opened last week, and I'm already making a profit."

"Really?" you ask.

"Really," he answers, passing you a couple more boxes of chips.

You're pretty impressed. You don't know anyone who came up with the idea for a business and then made it work.

"That's amazing," you tell him.

He shrugs after handing you a smaller box, this one filled with cookies. "My parents' restaurant is great," he says, "but I feel like there are ways to improve it, ways to expand it into something more successful. We do okay, but I know we can do better. I have lots of ideas."

"Like what?" you ask.

He jumps down from the back of the truck with

another box of cookies in his hand and stacks it on top of the rest of the boxes you've put on the dolly. Then he sits down on the truck bed and pats the spot next to him. You sit down and dangle your legs over the side.

"Like an army of these trucks, one at every beach that allows it. Like a more upscale restaurant on Main Street in town. Or maybe not upscale, but superspecialized. Like only lobster rolls, like the truck. Or maybe only steamers. And then make them the best in the whole area, you know?"

All those ideas sound great to you.

"Is this what you do full-time?" you ask. You're wondering now how old he is. He looks about your age, but the way he's talking makes you think he's out of college or something.

"No," he says, shaking his head. "I'm in high school. I'll be a junior in the fall. And then I want to get a business degree and a culinary degree and make my parents' restaurant as famous as the ones Bobby Flay owns."

"That sounds like a spectacular plan," you say. You're extra impressed now, knowing that he's the same age you are. You look at him and think that maybe this guy is one of the most incredible people you've ever met. He's handsome, he's charming, he's smart, he's passionate, he has this incredible life goal—and he seems really close to his family, too.

"So do *you* have a spectacular plan?" Jackson asks.

"Nothing as spectacular as that," you tell him. "I want to go to college. Maybe major in communications. Or psychology. I'm not really sure."

"Psychology," he says. "That's really interesting. And communications. Kind of two sides of the same thing. Interacting with people."

"Yeah," you say. "I guess it is. I think people are interesting. The way they act, the things they say, how what happened to them before affects them now."

"People *are* very interesting," he agrees. "You especially." He slides off the edge of the truck and opens up the top box of cookies. He slips a cigar-shaped one out of a wrapper and comes back toward you.

"Me especially?" you parrot.

"You liked my mom's cookie before?" he asks.

You nod. "It was delicious."

"Then you have to taste this one, too," he says. "Close your eyes and open your mouth."

You do, even though you feel a little silly doing it.

He slips the cookie inside, but before you can bite down, he says, "Let it melt in your mouth."

So you do. It's some sort of meringue that disintegrates on your tongue.

You open your eyes.

"Good?" he asks.

You nod.

"Can I have some, too?" he asks.

You nod again, but you're not sure what that means. Is he going to break off a piece of it while it's still in your mouth?

As his face moves closer to yours, you realize exactly what it means. He puts his lips around the cookie and up against yours. Then he bites off the piece of cookie that's sticking out of your mouth.

You chew what's left of your cookie and smile. "Cookie kiss?" you ask.

"Cookie kiss," he answers after swallowing his bite.

But you decide that just a cookie kiss isn't enough. You want more than that.

"Real kiss?" you ask.

He smiles and says, "Real kiss," as he leans over and kisses you softly.

His lips taste like cookies, and he smells like butter and lobster and beach.

You decide that Jackson is someone you could kiss like this over and over. Maybe even forever.

CONGRATULATIONS!
YOU'VE FOUND YOUR HAPPY ENDING!

YOU wave back to the fisherman.

"Two for two?" Tasha says to you. You figure, Why not?

"Sure," you say.

"Hey!" Tasha calls down to them from the boardwalk.

"Hey back!" the jean-shorts fisherman yells back. "You girls want to come down here?"

You look at Tasha. "Wanna?" she asks.

"Yeah, let's," you say. "Why not."

"That's what I like to hear!" Tasha says. "Happy birthday to you."

You laugh as the two of you get up to toss the trash from your lobster rolls and then head down the stairs to the fish-loading dock.

When you make it down, the two fishermen are

waiting for you. Also, it reeks of freshly caught fish.

"Sorry about the smell," cargo shorts says. "I'm Will, by the way."

You introduce yourself and then say, "This is my cousin Tasha."

"And I'm James," jean shorts says.

"You come here a lot?" Will asks you. And you have to laugh because it sounds like a pickup line from a movie.

He starts to laugh, too. "Sorry, I didn't realize how lame that sounded until I said it. But seriously, are you from around here?"

You laugh again, and so does Will. You wonder how many cheesy pickup lines he'll spout if you let him keep going. But you decide to spare him further embarrassment and answer his questions.

"I usually come about once a summer," you tell him, "to visit Tasha. She's here all summer long. Down the street." You gesture toward Tasha's house.

"All summer long?" James asks, tilting his head to the right, his eyes on Tasha.

She smiles back at him with her lips closed. "All summer long," she says.

"I think she just made his day," Will tells you. "Maybe his month. Or season."

"Dude!" James elbows Will.

These guys are hilarious. You and Tasha exchange a look—you can tell she's really enjoying this.

Then James clears his throat. "So we just finished on the boat and were thinking about having a Jet Ski race. Any chance you two want to be our lucky charms?"

You and Tasha exchange a look. You nod at her. Because, why not? You're only sixteen, celebrating your birthday at the beach, once.

"We'll see who's luckier," she says to you, and walks over to James. "Let's do this."

"So I guess I'm yours," you say to Will.

"I was hoping you would be," he answers. "And just so you know, I'm supercompetitive."

"Well then, we'll have to make sure we win. Is there anything I can do to make us go faster?"

He leads you to a Jet Ski with a white and silver bottom and a red top. There's a black lightning bolt down the side. He flips up the seat, and there are two life jackets underneath. He hands you one.

"We just have to be as streamlined as possible," he says, as he slips his life jacket on and zips it up. "Stay seated, keep your arms tight around me, and make sure your head is lower than mine."

"That should be easy," you say, looking up at him. He's at least five inches taller than you.

Tasha and James are at the Jet Ski next to Will's. It's hot green, yellow, and white. Not your favorite color combination. Tasha looks over at you as she's zipping herself into a hot green life jacket and gives you a thumbs-up. You give her one back.

"Ready?" James calls over.

"Ready!" Will calls back.

He helps you onto the back of the Jet Ski and then climbs on and unties the rope holding it to the dock. He clips a cord attached to his key to a hook on his life jacket and slides onto the seat in front of you.

"To the buoy and back?" he yells to James. "Like usual?"

"Like usual!" James yells back. "On my count."

Will inserts the key into the Jet Ski and waits.

"One," James yells.

Will turns the key in the ignition.

"Two!" James's voice is harder to hear over the engine.

Will puts his hands on the handlebars.

"Three!" James shouts.

Will squeezes the levers behind the handlebars and you're off.

The wind is whipping through your hair, and you hold on tighter to Will, feeling his muscles flex under your fingers.

"Woohoo!" he whoops as you speed forward and pass James and Tasha.

"Go, Will, go!" you shout.

He squeezes the levers harder, and you shoot forward again.

"We're so going to win!" you yell, as your hair whips you in the face and the smell of fish and ocean and boy fills your nostrils.

And just then you decide it doesn't matter if you win. It doesn't even matter if you see Will again after this Jet Ski race. But this, this wind-in-your-hair, anything-can-happen, exhilarating feeling is what it's all about. You get to live only once, and you decide then and there that you're going to make every moment of your life as exciting as possible.

CONGRATULATIONS!
YOU'VE FOUND YOUR HAPPY ENDING!

YOU take Jade's phone and look at her picture again. She really does look better than both of the actresses.

"Let's stay," you say to Tasha. "And Jade, if you're serious, I'd love a makeover!"

"Wait, for real?" Jade asks, sitting up straighter in her lounge chair.

You nod.

"Can I do anything?" she asks.

"Ja-a-ade," Tasha says, pulling her name out into a three-syllable warning.

"I mean, I won't, like, dye her hair purple or anything!"

"You can do anything within reason," you tell her. "Anything as long as it won't make my parents flip."

Jade gives you a once-over, as if you're an antique

dresser she might purchase for her dorm room. "How strict are your parents?" she asks.

"Medium strict," you say.

"Like mine," Tasha adds. "No purple hair, no eyebrow piercings, no tattoos, that sort of thing."

Jade nods. "Okay," she says, standing up. "We're done out here. Follow me to the locker room."

You walk downstairs into the locker room, which really resembles a plush relaxation room in a spa more than it does a locker room in a gym. There's a steam room, a hot tub that women are lounging in, and a sauna, plus glass pitchers filled with a mixture of water, ice, and cucumber slices.

"Okay, you take a shower," Jade tells you. "I'm going to ask the women in the spa for a few things. They know me."

Of course they know her! Jade has spent the last decade of summers at this country club. And you suspect a lot of that time was in the spa.

You go into one of the showers, and when you turn it on, there's water coming at you from four different showerheads, one on each side. There's also a little bench in there, but you're not sure why someone would need to sit in the middle of showering. You use the fancy shampoo and conditioner in dispensers on the wall, and when you're all soaped up and rinsed off, you use the plush towel and bathrobe you grabbed from a credenza in the bathroom.

When you poke your head into the changing area, Jade and Tasha are waiting for you.

"Oh good! You're ready!" Jade says, a huge smile on her face. "I cleared some things with the spa people and enlisted the help of some of the girls I know there. They're only a year or two older than Tash and me. Anyway, first I'm going to cut your hair, and then Lia's going to highlight it. After that Gabriela's going to dye your eyelashes. Then I'll do your makeup and we'll figure out clothes and stuff. I have some old dresses that I leave here for just in case, like if I've spent the day at the pool and Dex wants to go out afterward. I have a feeling there's something in that collection that'll be perfect for you!"

"You're cutting my hair?" you ask. "And highlighting it? And I've never heard of dyeing eyelashes."

"Just trust me," Jade says. "I swear you're going to look like you, but just enhanced. And I've been dyeing my eyelashes since I was fourteen."

Jade bats her eyelashes, and you notice that they do look pretty good.

"I did it at the end of last summer," Tasha tells you. "It's not a big deal at all."

Jade takes you into the hair salon area of the spa and turns you away from the mirror so you can't see what she's doing. She cuts and snips, but it doesn't seem too drastic. Then she looks at you critically.

"Short bangs?" she asks Tasha. But before Tasha can respond, Jade shakes her head. "Nah, I don't think you have the right face for it."

You're not sure what that means, but you're a little grateful for your face shape, because you're not so into bangs.

Instead of a fringe, Jade cuts a few short pieces around your face. "To frame it," she tells you, "and to bring people's attention to your eyes."

"Okay," you say, nodding. There's something kind of exciting about getting all of this done without knowing how it's going to look. It's like you're on a reality TV show or something.

Then a girl with purple streaks in her hair comes over and puts her hand out. "I'm Lia," she says. "Jade asked me to give you some highlights."

"Nothing too dramatic," Jade tells you and Lia together. "I just want it to look like she's spent the last month on the beach."

"Got it," Lia says, running her fingers through her own purple hair. "I know exactly what you mean."

She goes off to mix something together, and you wonder if you should maybe call your parents and make sure it's okay to get your hair highlighted. But then you decide it's better to do it and ask for forgiveness later than to ask for permission and have them say no. Besides, you're sixteen! That's certainly old enough to make decisions about your own hair. You can practically drive!

Lia brushes some goop into your hair, but you're still facing away from the mirror, so you can't tell what's going on.

"I think you're going to love this," she says. "It'll be really subtle; you'll look sun-kissed. Perfect for summer."

"Thanks," you say to her. "That sounds great."

When Lia's done, Jade has you follow her into a treatment room, where Gabriela is waiting to dye your eyelashes a dark black.

"This is the best invention," Jade tells you. "Like, even if you go out without makeup on, you're basically still wearing mascara. It's so good for, like, the gym and the summer when you want to go swimming or if you get sweaty. You won't end up with raccoon eyes."

That, of course, immediately makes you wonder if you've had raccoon eyes all day and nobody's told you. But then you figure Tasha would've told you for sure. She'd never let you walk around with makeup smudged on your face.

Gabriela puts wet cotton balls underneath your eyes and then tells you to close them. She paints something on your lashes and then tells you to relax for a few minutes while the dye is working.

"If it stings, just give a holler," she says.

You don't think she means it about the hollering, and you really hope it won't sting. But maybe that's the price of beauty?

A few minutes—and no stinging—later, Gabriela is back and wiping the excess dye off your lashes. Then Jade appears and whisks you back to the hair salon, where Lia takes out the foil your highlights were wrapped in. "How do you want it blown?" she asks.

"I'll do that part," Jade says. "I just need a round brush and a dryer."

Lia raises her eyebrows. "Okay," she says, "if that's what you want."

"It is," Jade confirms.

You close your eyes while Jade pulls and blows

and brushes you. The heat from the blow-dryer is intense, but Jade never holds it to your scalp for longer than you can handle. The blow-out feels pretty professional, in fact.

After Jade turns the dryer off, you look up at Tasha, and she's smiling. "Oh, you're so going to love this," she says.

"Close your eyes!" Jade commands, and you do.

Then she turns your chair around so you're facing the mirror and says, "Open!"

When you open your eyes, it looks like the very best version of yourself is staring back at you in the mirror. Your hair has body and bounce to it, but it looks totally natural, not styled at all. And Lia was right, the highlights are really subtle—it does look like you spent a month on the beach and the sun kissed your hair. And your eyes! They're framed by thick, dark lashes.

"Wow!" you say. "You seriously are good at this, Jade."

"We're not done yet!" she says.

She takes you down to a different part of the salon and sweeps creams and powders on your face and, before she lets you look, heads to her locker, which is really more like a small closet, and gives you a drapey green silk dress. "I think this will look perfect on you, and it never really looked quite right on me anyway."

You put it on, and then Jade pulls a bracelet and necklace out of a pouch in her locker. "These are on loan," she says. "And keep your earrings on. Studs are in."

You slip on her jewelry.

"Okay," she says. "Now you can look."

You walk over to a mirror with Jade and Tasha trailing you. And you stare. And stare. In this dress, with that makeup and that hair, you look as if you could be in Tasha's magazine. You look like a movie star.

"Oh my gosh," you say. "I can't believe it's me! Thank you so much, Jade!"

"It wasn't just me. You gave me great material to work with."

You can feel yourself blush, but you're not sure if anyone can see it through your makeup.

"So," Tasha says, "now that you're all dressed, should we head out and see about flirting with some boys?"

You look at your new self in the mirror again.

"Actually," you say, "can we see what Lia and

Gabriela are doing tonight? How about we all get dressed and have a girls' night on the town? We don't need to dress up for boys, we can just dress up for us."

Jade puts her fist out and you bump it. "I like how you're thinking," she says. "I'll talk to Lia and Gabriela. Girls' night out. And no worries about boys to ruin it!"

"Awesome," you say. There's always time to think about boys, if you want to. Tonight, you're just going to think about how fantastic it is to have great girlfriends with fabulous fashion skills and a beautiful summer night to spend with them.

CONGRATULATIONS!
YOU'VE FOUND YOUR HAPPY ENDING!

THERE'S something very intriguing about Mitch. He's got dark hair cropped close to his head and surprisingly light blue eyes. So light they look almost silver. And he's clearly interested in you.

You look back at Dex. He's pretty awesome, too. You suppress a tiny laugh thinking about all these handsome tennis-playing boys. When you came out for the weekend, you had no idea this would happen!

You decide that if Dex steps in and refuses to switch partners, you'll stay with him, but if not, you'll switch sides and see what the story is with Mitch.

"So what do you think?" Mila asks. "A partner swap?"

Dex rolls his eyes at her. "I'm cool with whatever. I just want to play."

"Hey!" you say, slightly bummed. "Clearly I'm not wanted on this side. I'll come play with you, Mitch."

"I didn't mean that!" Dex says.

"Your loss, man." Mitch smiles. "Welcome to the sunny side of the court," he says once you walk around the net and switch places with Mila.

You start playing again, and you realize that this pairing is actually much better. Mitch is a stronger player than his sister, but Dex makes up for Mila's shortcomings on the court. It also seems as if Dex has slowed down his serve slightly, because you're able to return most of them.

You give it your all and play pretty well. Your high school tennis coach would be proud. More than proud, she might actually be impressed. Dex and Mila win the first set. You and Mitch win the second. And now it's the third set, match point, and you're serving.

"Forty–fifteen!" you say.

You toss the ball, stretch your racket just like Dex did, and slam the ball with the perfect combination of power and spin. It whips right by Mila.

"Game, set, match!" Mitch cheers, running over to you. Before you realize what's happening, he lifts you up in the air and spins you around. "So, any chance I can persuade you to stay all summer?" he asks. "It's rare we can find someone who can beat Dex."

"If she stays, she's mine!" Dex says. "I wasn't

giving away my partner for good."

You put your hands on your hips. "Oh, I see how it is. You didn't care before, but now that I can beat you, you don't want me playing with Mitch!" You're not actually angry with him, but maybe a little miffed. Especially because of the giving-my-partner-away line, as if you were something he owned and could loan out.

"Oooh, you got her mad now! She's mine for sure." Mitch holds his hand out to you. "May I interest you in a lemonade before our next match?" The players on court five haven't finished their match yet, so the four of you have some time to kill before playing again.

"Forget lemonade, how about a virgin piña colada at the bar?" Dex asks. "I didn't mean to . . . mean to . . ."

"Make her mad?" Mila offers.

"Exactly!" Dex grins at you, kind of flirty, kind of chagrined.

If you go with Dex, turn to page 53.

- - - - -

If you go with Mitch, turn to page 175.

- - - - -

*If you'd rather sit and watch your
competition, turn to page 181.*

BEFORE you can say anything, Dex speaks up. "No way," he says. "You dance with the girl you came with; it's the gentlemanly thing to do, guys. Besides"—now he's looking right at you—"I came with a pretty spectacular girl. Why would I want someone else to dance with her?"

You can feel yourself blushing, and you look down at your tennis shoes, hoping Dex won't be able to see how pink your cheeks have turned.

"What if she doesn't want to stay partnered with you, man?" Mitch asks, twirling his racket in his hands.

You look up, and then look over at Dex. He's clearly waiting for you to answer. "You dance with the guy you came with," you tell Mitch. "It's the ladylike thing to do. Besides, I came with a pretty spectacular guy. Why would I want someone else to dance with him?"

Dex laughs at your echo of his words. "So are we playing?" he asks.

"Fine," Mila says, "but it's no fun when you know you're going to lose."

"You never know what's going to happen in tennis," Dex says, bouncing the ball with his racket. "Ready?"

"Ready," the twins both say.

You try not to play too aggressively, because Mila is right about games being no fun when one team can really outplay the other, and you can tell Dex is holding back, too. But even with that, you beat them pretty quickly and pretty solidly.

You and Dex head to the net to shake hands with Mitch and Mila.

"I need lemonade," Mila announces, and heads off the court.

"Ditto," Mitch says, following his sister.

"Do you want lemonade, too?" Dex asks.

Lemonade actually does sound pretty great—but before you can answer, Dex says, "Wait! I have a better idea. Virgin piña coladas from the bar!"

You smile. That does sound like a better idea.

"Deal," you say. "We should celebrate our win before we have to play the next match."

"You got it," Dex says. He takes your racket and leans it up against the fence on court four with his, and then leads you upstairs.

Turn to page 193.

YOU look at Dex. He is really cute, and you thought that maybe there was some good chemistry between you, but he also didn't seem to care if he played mixed doubles with you. And the way he talked about giving you away like you were an object was really unappealing.

Then you look at Mitch. You remember what it felt like to have him spin you around. You think about the fact that he wanted to keep you around all summer.

You take the hand Mitch has held out to you and say, "A lemonade sounds quite lovely!"

"Oooh," Mila says. "Harsh. But I'll go get a virgin piña colada with you, Dex. Just so you don't get too sad."

Dex concentrates on rewrapping the tape on his

racket's grip. "I think I'll just hang here," he says, "and fix my racket. But you're welcome to hang with me, Mila."

"Sure," she says. "I'll help."

Leaving the two of them behind, Mitch leads you just off the court to a cooler of lemonade. He fills two plastic cups, hands you one, then perches on the top of the fence. You hop up next to him.

"You're a kick-butt tennis player," he says, taking a sip of his lemonade.

"Thanks," you say, after swallowing a sip of yours. "You're good, too."

He shakes his head. "Not as good as Dex. That kid dominates. At everything. It's kind of infuriating. I've been competing with him for years—tennis, lacrosse, track—he's always number one, and I'm always number two. It kills me."

You study Mitch for a second. "Well, as far as I'm concerned, you're number one and he's number two today."

Mitch turns to look at you, and his silver-blue eyes flash in the sunlight.

"Your eyes are incredible," you tell him. "They make you look superhuman."

"Oh . . . you mean no one's told you that my sister and I are vampires?" he asks you, with a serious look on his face. "We're wearing special sunscreen so we don't sparkle."

You can't help but laugh at that, and with a mouth full of lemonade, some of it comes snorting out of your nose. You quickly swallow the rest and swipe at the liquid dripping down onto your lip. How humiliating! "Oh God," you say. "I can't believe that just happened! I'm so embarrassed."

Mitch grabs a paper towel from a stack next to the lemonade cooler. "No need to be embarrassed," he says, handing you one. "Would it be embarrassing if I told you I thought it was kind of adorable?"

You squint at him. "You think it's adorable when lemonade comes out of someone's nose?"

"No." He shakes his head. "Not anyone's nose. Just your nose. You know, I was trying to figure out how to get you to be my tennis partner ever since I saw you at lunch. I'm glad you gave Mila and me an excuse to suggest it."

"Your sister was in on this plan?" You can't believe all the prep work he did to get to hang with you.

"My sister's in on all my plans," he says. "She's a great co-conspirator."

The way he says it makes you wish that you had a twin brother. "Yeah?" you ask.

"Well, you're here with me now, aren't you?"

You laugh again. This time no lemonade drips out of your nose. "Fair point," you tell him.

"I do have one more plan I'd like to enact today," he says, sliding a little closer to you on the fence.

You feel your heart speed up. He's going to kiss you. That has to be his plan. For a split second you wonder if you want him to, but then you decide, Why not? He's nice and funny, and a great athlete, even though he seems to have a weird complex about Dex. But he saw lemonade come out of your nose and still thinks you're cute, so that has to count for something.

"And what plan is that?" you ask, as you feel your palms getting sweaty.

"This one," he says, closing his eyes as he moves his face toward yours.

You lean forward to meet his mouth, and then close your own eyes.

His lips are softer and smoother than you expected them to be. His hand on the small of your back pulls you in closer. He flicks the tip of his tongue into your mouth for a tiny second, and when it's gone all you can think about is wanting it to come back. You press yourself closer to him and reach one of your hands up to rub the prickles of his crew cut.

Then you hear someone clear her throat. You and Mitch break apart, and Mila is standing there. "They sent me to tell you guys that the other match is over," she says. "It's time to play again."

You look down, a little embarrassed that Mitch's sister just caught the two of you mid–make out, but Mitch doesn't seem to mind. He grabs your hand, interlacing his fingers with yours.

"We'll be right there," he tells Mila.

She fills her water bottle from the watercooler next to the lemonade and heads back to the court.

"Are you okay?" Mitch asks.

You nod. "More than okay," you tell him.

"Good," he whispers. "Then let's win this one so we can celebrate with another kiss."

"Deal," you tell him, and squeeze his hand. But as you head back to the court, you wonder how you're going to keep your mind on the game when all you can think about is kissing Mitch.

CONGRATULATIONS!
YOU'VE FOUND YOUR HAPPY ENDING!

YOU look at both guys and realize neither one of them is really all that attractive. At least not personality-wise. True, agreeing to get lemonade or a piña colada doesn't mean agreeing to anything more, but why spend your time hanging out with guys who haven't really impressed you very much?

"I think," you say, eyeing the game on court five, "I'm going to stay here and check out the competition. If Mitch and I are going to win again, I may need to take some notes."

"I like that competitive spirit," Mitch says. "Want me to grab you some water?"

You nod, and he and Mila go off to the water-cooler. Dex starts wrapping the grip on his racket with new tape. You busy yourself watching the group of four playing next to you and quickly realize that you and Mitch will be able to take either pair, no problem. Actually, so will Mila and Dex.

Mitch comes back with the water, and you thank him before chugging it down. It's ice cold and perfect on such a hot day.

"So," Mitch says, sitting down next to you, "we gonna beat them?"

You nod. "Absolutely."

Soon the game on court five ends, and you and Mitch start playing against Silas and Greta, who, you find out, have been dating since seventh grade. You win in two sets, the last one a bagel. And Dex and Mila win their game, no problem.

After you all shake hands across the net, Silas and Greta announce that they're going for ice cream. Mitch and Mila have to go meet up with their parents. Dex decides to go to the driving range. And the last doubles pair, Primo and Tala, want to go over to the bar for some virgin daiquiris. They invite you to join, but you decide to head to the pool to see what Tasha and Jade are up to.

Continue to page 23.

DINNER? Jazz festival? Adam? Yes, yes, and yes!

You know Tasha is probably planning on hanging out with you tonight, but you also know that if you bail for boy reasons, she won't mind. Plus, she's always happy to go out with Jade.

"That sounds fun," you tell Adam. He smiles, and you smile back, already looking forward to spending more time with him.

"So I'll pick you up at seven," he says. "I'll be in my mom's lame station wagon—I hope that's okay."

You laugh. "Of course that's okay! I don't care what kind of car you drive."

You give him Tasha's parents' address, and the two of you head back to the pool holding hands. When you reach the pool gate, he looks down at his watch.

"I've got to get the triplets in a minute, but I don't

think I can wait until later to do this."

"Do what?" you ask.

"This," he says again, as he tips your chin up so you're looking him in the eye. The pull he has on you feels irresistible, and you lean toward him. He bends down and presses his warm lips against yours. He tastes sweet, like Sprite. You wrap your arms around his neck, and he lifts you up so your feet are dangling a few inches off the ground and your body is tight against his. You've always kissed with your eyes closed, but this time you open them and look at his tan skin and perfectly straight eyelashes.

Still holding you up, he pulls his mouth away from yours and opens his eyes.

"See you later," he says softly, as he lowers you down to the ground.

"See you later," you say back.

Then he heads to the pool to collect the triplets. And you take a moment to collect yourself before following. You were looking for a fun guy to flirt with, but you're pretty sure you've found something more.

CONGRATULATIONS!
YOU'VE FOUND YOUR HAPPY ENDING!

AS much fun as you're having with Adam, you're not sure about going out with him later. You like him too much for him to be a one-night fling, and you're worried that with his job and his plans and his living so far away, the two of you don't really have a chance at something real. It's better to say no. Safer to say no. And besides, you don't want to ditch Tasha, even if she'd probably understand.

"I wish I could," you say, "but I'm hanging out with my cousin tonight."

"That's too bad," he says as you head back toward the pool. "Maybe another time?"

"Maybe," you say. For a minute you wonder if you should change your mind, but then you decide to stick to the choice you made. There are so many guys around this summer, and Adam's not right for you. At least not right now.

Continue to page 187.

TASHA and Jade have finished talking about their dorm room decoration, and now they're looking at a "Who Wore It Best?" article in one of Tasha's magazines.

"I totally have this!" Jade squeals, pointing to a cobalt blue drapey dress that two B-list actresses wore to different movie premieres the week before.

Tasha inspects the pictures closely. "Did you wear it with peep-toes like this one, or gladiators, like that one?" she asks Jade.

"Ugh, neither." Jade waves her hand as if she's fanning away a bad smell. "Strappy gold sandals with heels. I wore it to the prom after-party."

You look at the pictures yourself, over Tasha's shoulder. "If you wore it with strappy gold sandals, I think you probably wore it better than both of these girls."

"Totally," Tasha says. "How did you wear your hair? And what jewelry? I feel like that's always the most important after shoes."

Jade reaches into her tote and pulls out her phone. She scrolls through the pictures and lands on one of her in the blue dress with her gold sandals, her hair in a high, curled ponytail with some height in the front, and a thin gold necklace around her neck with a diamond nestled in the hollow of her throat. She had diamond studs in her ears and three bangles on her right wrist: two gold and a cobalt blue one that matched the dress almost perfectly.

"Oh, you totally wore it best," Tasha says after looking at the picture and zooming in to see Jade's jewelry better.

"Absolutely," you say. "I mean, seriously, you should've been their stylist. And they should fire the one they have."

"You know that's what I want to do after college, right?" Jade says to you. "Be a stylist?"

You shake your head. "I didn't know, but I think you'd be amazing."

Jade leans back against her chaise lounge.

"Thanks," she said. "It's really my favorite thing to do, you know, putting outfits together, helping people look their best." Then she looks at you critically. "If you want, I could do you."

Tasha bonks Jade's knee with the magazine. "Leave my cousin alone—she looks great the way she is."

You hadn't actually been offended, though. It might be fun to have someone tell you what to wear to make you look best.

"So, cuz," Tasha says, turning to you, "have you had enough of this country club thing? Want to go to the beach now? I bet there'll be more boys for you to meet. . . ."

"Or you guys can stick here with me," Jade adds. "Because I've gotta meet my mom in a couple of hours in the spa. And even if you do look beautiful the way you are, I bet I could give you some tips that would make you look even *more* beautiful. . . ."

*Turn to page 203 if you decide
to go to the beach.*

- - - - -

*Turn to page 157 if you decide
to stay with Jade.*

"SO why didn't you go with him?" Tasha asks.

You shrug. "I don't know, I guess I didn't want to talk about that guy getting hurt anymore, and I had a feeling he'd want to."

"He was cute," Tasha says.

"I know," you answer, "but there'll be other cute guys around."

Tasha nods. "Yeah. Want to grab something to eat? Or maybe head back home? I'm kind of done with the sand-and-ocean thing right now."

After all the excitement down here, you find yourself agreeing with Tasha. Enough with the sand and ocean for the moment.

*Turn to page 211 if you
decide to grab some food.*

- - - - -

*Turn to page 15 if you'd
rather head home.*

YOU get to the bar that's overlooking the tennis courts, and Dex orders you both virgin piña coladas. They arrive with mini-umbrellas and a wedge of pineapple on top.

"These are my favorite," he says. "It's like summertime in a cup."

You take a sip and realize he's right. The mixture of coconut, pineapple, and icy coldness tastes like everything summer should be—sweet, tart, nutty, and delicious.

"This is phenomenal," you tell Dex. "Thank you."

He smiles and takes another swallow of his drink. It looks as if maybe he's building up courage for something.

"Do you want to try something even more phenomenal?" he asks.

You quirk one eyebrow up at him, trying to master Tasha's eyebrow communication. Could this mean what you think it means? "It depends what it is," you say, hoping your smile tells him that if the more phenomenal thing is a kiss, you're totally game.

It must work, because without any more words, Dex leans in and kisses you hard on the mouth, sliding his tongue between your lips. He tastes salty and sweet and tart and nutty and delicious. "It's that," he says, pulling away from you for a second.

"You were right," you tell him, slightly breathless. "That was phenomenal."

You can tell he's a little breathless, too, but he gives you a lazy half smile and kisses you again, slower this time.

When he stops, he says, "You have no idea how long I've been wanting to do that."

"Really?" you ask.

"Really," he says. "For at least three years. Since the summer you had that white bathing suit with the ruffles."

You remember that bathing suit. And that summer. "I had no idea," you tell him.

He kisses you again. "But now you do."

"Yes," you say, your mouth barely an inch from his, "now I do."

Soon your drinks are forgotten, and you let yourself relax into his arms, tasting his lips and feeling them warm up as they press against yours. After a few more kisses you decide that kissing Dex is much, much better than kissing Tyler Grant ever could be. Especially when he tastes like summer.

CONGRATULATIONS!
YOU'VE FOUND YOUR HAPPY ENDING!

"WALK, bike, or car?" Tasha asks, as she throws a hat, sunglasses, some magazines, a book, and an iPod into her tote.

"Walk," you answer, and pack up your own tote.

Tasha's house is on a street that has its own private beach for everyone who lives there. The beach is kind of fantastic and is only about a six-minute walk away. (Biking takes three minutes. And driving takes about one.)

Once you get to the beach, you and Tasha survey the sand. There's an open space down close to the water, but Tasha had a bad experience with high tide the summer before—when it came in superfast and carried her favorite Ray-Bans out to sea—so you opt not to take that one.

"How about the spot by the lifeguard stand?" Tasha asks.

You look up at the lifeguard. There's definite flirt potential there. "Looks good to me," you say.

You and Tasha lay out your towels side by side and stick your flip-flops and bags in strategic spots to stop the towels from blowing away in the wind. Your eyes keep zipping up to the lifeguard, but his eyes are on the ocean. He's clearly a very responsible guy. Usually, that would be a mark in his favor, but not when it keeps him from noticing you!

You rummage around in your bag and pull out your book. It's one that's on your summer reading list for school, but it's not half bad. It's about this guy who wakes up one morning and he's a bug.

Tasha looks over at you. "You're reading *The Metamorphosis* at the beach?" she asks.

You shrug. "Good a place as any to read it."

"Beach books are supposed to be, you know, about summer and friendships and weddings and things like that. See?" She pulls a book out of her bag with an ocean and sand and a beach chair on the cover. "This is a beach book."

You look around at the other people on their

towels. You point to a man about your dad's age about four spots over to your left. "That guy's reading a very fat book that looks like it's nonfiction," you say. "About wars."

"Guys are different," she tells you.

You shake your head. "You're being ridiculous. I'm reading my bug book at the beach."

She sighs. "I think I'm going to go swimming."

"Because I won't stop reading my bug book?" you ask.

She tightens her ponytail. "No, because the ocean looks beautiful, and it's hotter than Grandpa's barbecue sauce out here." She pauses, probably thinking about your shared grandpa's barbecue sauce, which totally once gave someone a lip blister. "But you and the bug book aren't giving me a reason to stay on this towel."

You roll your eyes. "Go swim in the ocean. My bug book and I will be fine here on this towel all alone."

Tasha heads toward the ocean, and you get back to reading. But before you've even finished a chapter, the lifeguard behind you blows his whistle and then comes flying off his chair. A woman down by the shoreline starts screaming. You follow the lifeguard with your eyes and see him dive into the ocean. He takes a few steady strokes, goes under, and comes up with something under his arm. You stand up to see if it's a person. It looks as if maybe it is. A smallish person. With long hair.

You can't believe the lifeguard just rescued someone in front of your eyes! Except as he gets closer you realize it's not a person. It's a golden retriever. The cute, responsible lifeguard just rescued someone's dog. This makes you like him even more.

You watch as he returns the dog to an older woman who looks as if she maybe could be someone's grandma. She grabs onto the dog's collar and starts shouting at it. Then she's hugging it. And then she's hugging the lifeguard. You take a few steps back to your towel and sit down, watching people slap the lifeguard on the back and high-five him as he heads back to his chair.

While he's walking, you notice how ripped he is. Amazing pecs. Really cut arms and legs. You know it takes a lot to be an ocean guard, and this guy looks as if he's more than strong enough.

You let your gaze travel up to his eyes and you

find them looking right at you. Coffee-bean dark and deep, like there are secrets in those eyes. He smiles. You smile back. Then he keeps walking and climbs up on his chair.

You look at the bug book in front of you. Then you look over to the lifeguard stand. After a look like that, you wonder if you should go over and see if he wants to talk—or flirt.

---

*Turn to page 35 if you decide to
get back to reading*
The Metamorphosis.

- - - - -

*Turn to page 37 if you decide to walk
over to the lifeguard stand and say hello.*

AS much fun as it would be to get prettied up by Jade, the boys at the beach seem like a more exciting way to spend your birthday weekend. And since Dex is nowhere to be found, you and Tasha call a cab to come take you home.

"I so wish I had my car out here," Tasha says, as she pays the cabby and steps out onto her parents' pebbled driveway.

"We could've driven," you say, shrugging. "I said I would be your map reader and iPod manager."

"And get stuck in all that traffic?" She shakes her head. "We made the right choice. More vacation time this way. But I still wish I had my car here."

You drop your big bag on the floor in the kitchen

and pull out a tote to pack up. You are so ready for the beach.

Continue to page 197.

"GUYS are jerks," she says, flopping down on her towel and wringing salt water from her hair.

"What happened?" you ask, sitting down cross-legged next to her.

"So I met this adorable guy in the water," she says, "and we got into a splash fight, and then we were dunking each other, and he took, like, every opportunity possible to touch me, and then just now, like, so long into the whole flirty business, he mentions his effing girlfriend. Who *does* that? Who meets a new girl in the ocean and plays around with her and then has an effing *girlfriend*!"

"A jerk," you say. "A total jerk."

"A total complete one hundred percent effing jerk." Tasha leans back so the sun can hit her body directly and dry her suit. "How was your time on the towel?"

You shrug. "Not too eventful. But on the plus side, I didn't flirt with any guys who have girlfriends."

Tasha groans. Then she says, "Are you hungry? I'm hungry."

You take a moment to take stock of things. "Not really," you say. "But I'll take a walk with you if you want to get something."

"Oh good!" Tasha says. "Let me grab flip-flops and a cover-up, and we can go to the food trucks in the parking lot."

"I thought you weren't into food made in a moving vehicle," you say. Tasha has had a thing against food trucks since they started inundating the city you both live in. You don't share her opinion and happen to like a bunch of them, especially the one that makes waffles.

"I'm not usually," Tasha says, as you both start heading over to the parking lot, "but Jade said that the guy who runs the lobster-roll truck is adorable and really sweet. And my love of adorable non-jerky guys is stronger than my dislike of kitchens on wheels."

"Fair enough," you say.

You get to the parking lot and see four food trucks—the lobster-roll one, a fro-yo one, a hot-dog one, and traditional Mister Softee. If you got anything, you'd get that. A swirl of soft-serve chocolate rolled in chocolate sprinkles. But you're a good cousin, so you stand with Tasha in the lobster-roll line.

"Did you see the menu?" she asks. "There are, like, seven different options! I thought there was only one kind of lobster roll."

"I knew about two," you say. "The one with mayo, and the one with butter."

"Hmm, interesting," Tasha says. But she's clearly focused on the menu and not you.

Your eyes start to wander, and you notice the guy working the lobster-roll truck. He is all kinds of adorable with freckles and spiked hair and eyes the color of blueberries. You also see one of those chalkboard signs with two sides to it. The side facing you says, NEW! SURF SCHOOL! JEAN PAUL FROM BIARRITZ WILL TEACH YOU TO SURF! You are very intrigued.

"Did Jade mention anything about the new surf school?" you ask Tasha.

She shakes her head. "But Jade isn't so much into

swimming in the ocean, so she might've ignored it."

"How could she ignore it if there's a French instructor from Biarritz named Jean Paul?"

Tasha laughs. "True. If she'd seen that, I bet she would've explored and been able to give us a full report."

The lobster-roll line moves, and you take a couple of steps forward. There are about five people between you and Mr. Blueberry Eyes now. He looks up briefly, as if he's checking out the length of the line, and his eyes catch yours. Your gazes lock, and he smiles for a millisecond before getting back to work.

"You should explore," Tasha says, elbowing you. "Maybe Jean Paul is your birthday kiss!"

"Just flirt," you remind her. "Not necessarily a kiss. And I thought we were here to check out the lobster-roll guy, who, by the way, just smiled at me."

Tasha raises both eyebrows. "So many boys, so little time!"

Turn to page 89 if you decide to wait in line to get a lobster roll.

- - - - -

Turn to page 93 to sign up for surf school.

YOU look at Marco one last time, and decide that a point on the flirting challenge is enough for now. Besides, you realize that Tasha has been gone for a big chunk of the afternoon, and you're starting to get a little worried.

"Thanks," you say, "but I think I should probably go find my cousin and make sure she's okay. I haven't seen her for hours, which is actually a little concerning, come to think of it."

Marco nods. "I totally understand," he says. "But if you change your mind, I'll be over here with Homer." He taps his book and you smile. Then you head back to your towel and start to scan the ocean for Tasha's bright yellow bikini. Just as soon as you do, though, you see her walking out of the ocean, making a beeline for you.

Continue to page 205.

YOU decide food might be the way to go. Maybe a small snack. Or at least a cold bottle of water.

"Let's check out the food," you say, grabbing your wallet.

You get to the parking lot and see four food trucks—a lobster-roll one, a fro-yo one, a hot-dog one, and the traditional Mister Softee. If you got anything, you'd get that. A swirl of soft-serve chocolate rolled in chocolate sprinkles. But you're a good cousin, so you stand in line with Tasha, who has decided she wants a lobster roll.

"Did you see the menu?" she asks. "There are, like, seven different options! I thought there was only one kind of lobster roll."

"I know about two," you say. "The one with mayo, and the one with butter."

"Hmm, interesting," Tasha says. But she's clearly focused on the menu and not you.

Your eyes start to wander, and you notice the guy working the lobster-roll truck. He is all kinds of adorable with freckles and spiked hair and eyes the color of blueberries. All of a sudden you're in the mood for blueberry pancakes. But there aren't any of those trucks around.

The lobster-roll line moves, and you take a couple of steps forward. There are about five people between you and Lobster Roll Guy now. He looks up briefly, as if he's checking out the length of the line, and his eyes catch yours. Your gazes lock, and he smiles for a millisecond before getting back to work.

"Someone likes you!" Tasha says. "And he looks tasty."

You roll your eyes. "He was just figuring out how many customers he has."

"I don't know about that," Tasha answers.

You decide to ignore her.

Continue to page 89.

FRISBEE Guy stops and turns around. "Are you sure? Anything I can do to get you to play?" he says.

"I don't even know your name," you tell him.

"Rafe," he answers, holding out his hand for you to shake.

You shake it and tell him your name.

"So," Rafe says, "you coming?"

As he says it, he rakes his fingers through his hair, and you see his biceps bulge. For a second, all you can think about is wrapping your hand around those muscles and feeling them move beneath your fingertips. He smiles at you, and you feel your stomach flip. That clinches it.

"Sure," you say. "I'll come."

You toss a sweatshirt over your bag and Tasha's, but you figure no one is really going to steal anything from a spot right beneath a lifeguard on a private beach anyway.

"Race you?" Rafe asks, looking as if he's about to take off down the beach.

"Deal," you answer, landing lightly on the sand as you run.

You sprint as fast as you can without your running shoes on, and Rafe matches you stride for stride. After a few steps in synch, you realize he's not really racing you at all. He's running completely by your side.

When you get to his group of friends, he stops and so do you.

"It's a tie!" he says, barely breathing hard.

"You totally could've beaten me," you tell him, trying to catch your breath.

His honey-colored eyes twinkle. "Well, we'll have to try again later, won't we?"

He smiles, and you smile back, that stomach flip happening again. Then he turns to his friends and introduces you. "She's got a great arm," he adds.

Rafe and another guy named Jonah are captains, and Rafe chooses you on his first pick. Jonah chooses another girl who's way taller and buffer than you are. One by one, everyone gets a spot on a team, and then Jonah paces in one direction while Rafe paces in the other, and they make themselves an Ultimate Frisbee field, outlining it with grooves in the sand.

"You know the rules?" one of your other teammates asks.

You nod, feeling thankful that your neighbor twisted your arm into playing on his team so often. You're not fantastic, but you're not an embarrassment, either.

"We play one-on-one," he says. "And the girl who's not here today usually covers Crystal." He's pointing to the buff girl from before. You take a deep breath. You can totally take her. Maybe.

When Rafe and Jonah finish making the field, the two teams split up and the game starts. Rafe tosses the Frisbee from your side of the field to Jonah's team, and then they start running and tossing, trying to get to the end zone back where Rafe started. You shadow Crystal, but the Frisbee doesn't come her way until you all get close to the end zone. One of the guys on the team throws it to her and you leap with her into the air, but she's so much taller than you that she grabs the Frisbee before your hand is even close.

You both land, and you see that she's looking

toward the end zone, trying to find someone to toss it to. You know she has only ten seconds, so you quickly try to see where she might throw it. Everyone seems to be covered in the end zone, and then you notice that Jonah's not there. He's behind Crystal and to her left! You realize this just as she does, and go racing toward him just as she throws the Frisbee, hoping you'll be able to stop it once it gets closer to him. Your legs are pumping and your eye is on the white plastic disc as it flies through the air. You can tell you're going to get there in time and catapult yourself up into the air to reach for the Frisbee.

You don't realize, though, that Rafe, who was covering Jonah, is heading for the Frisbee, too. You don't see each other at all, in fact, and both of you fly toward the white disc, both get a hand on it, and then both fall to the ground, the Frisbee between you.

"Oof," you say as you roll toward him.

"'Oof' is right," he says, his nose less than two inches from yours. "But we caught it."

You laugh. You're so close to Rafe that you feel as if you have to whisper. "Good for us," you say quietly.

"Yeah," he whispers back, and you see his breath move the sand between you just the tiniest bit.

All of a sudden the air feels electric, and Rafe's

eyes are locked onto yours. You feel certain that right there, on the sand, in the middle of an Ultimate game, Rafe is going to kiss you.

But then someone in the end zone yells, "Get up already!" and the lock between your eyes breaks. You let go of the Frisbee, and Rafe stands up holding it. Then he leans down and offers you his hand to help you up. You grab it and feel a tingle start in your fingers and work its way through your body. Once you're on your feet he says quietly, "Let's finish that later."

You try to not to smile too much while you say, "Absolutely."

He winks at you. "But first, we have a game to win."

So you focus on winning a game of Ultimate while imagining what will happen afterward . . . and decide that getting hit on the head with a Frisbee might have been the best thing to happen to you all day. Well, until Rafe kisses you, that is.

CONGRATULATIONS!
YOU'VE FOUND YOUR HAPPY ENDING!

ACKNOWLEDGMENTS

Special thanks to all the Penguins for their support on this project—most especially Don Weisberg, Jen Loja, Eileen Kreit, Jen Bonnell, Dana Bergman, and Michael Green. Special thanks, too, to my non-Penguin friends and family who listened to me go on about this book and offered their thoughts and opinions—especially Jenn Sapir and David Bell for their notes on dialogue-, tennis-, and lifeguard-related matters. I'd choose the path that leads to all of you every single time.